D0842543

WOMEN OF THE BIBLE

WOMEN OF THE BIBLE

Deborah's Story

A NN B URTON

**Doubleday Large Print
Home Library Edition**

A SIGNET BOOK

This Large Print Edition, prepared especially for Doubleday Large Print Home Library, contains the complete, unabridged text of the original Publisher's Edition.

SIGNET

Published by New American Library, a division of Penguin Group (USA) Inc., 375 Hudson Street, New York, New York 10014, USA • Penguin Group (Canada), 90 Eglinton Avenue East, Suite 700, Toronto, Ontario M4P 2Y3, Canada (a division of Pearson Penguin Canada Inc.) • Penguin Books Ltd., 80 Strand, London WC2R 0RL, England • Penguin Ireland, 25 St. Stephen's Green, Dublin 2, Ireland (a division of Penguin Books Ltd.) • Penguin Group (Australia), 250 Camberwell Road, Camberwell, Victoria 3124, Australia (a division of Pearson Australia Group Pty. Ltd.) • Penguin Books India Pvt. Ltd., 11 Community Centre, Panchsheel Park, New Delhi - 110 017, India • Penguin Group (NZ), cnr Airborne and Rosedale Roads, Albany, Auckland 1310, New Zealand (a division of Pearson New Zealand Ltd.) • Penguin Books (South Africa) (Pty.) Ltd., 24 Sturdee Avenue, Rosebank, Johannesburg 2196, South Africa

Penguin Books Ltd., Registered Offices:
80 Strand, London WC2R 0RL, England

First published by Signet, an imprint of New American Library, a division of Penguin Group (USA) Inc.

ISBN 13: 978-0-7394-7303-0

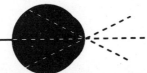

**This Large Print Book carries the
Seal of Approval of N.A.V.H.**

PART ONE

Song of Jeth

CHAPTER
1

It was through a lush and green garden that I walked, pausing occasionally to admire a bloom. Such fragile things flowers were, and yet here they burst forth as a thousand shofar, trumpeting their colors and beguiling the nose with their sweet scents. Morning dew kissed my toes, and birds chirped merrily to me from their perches in the labyrinth of cedar branches overhead.

I loved this place, and came here whenever I could.

Someone had built a fountain in the center of the garden, and that was where I walked now. It was a marvelous wonder, carved of polished ivory stone. The water splashing in the basin bubbled up from a hidden spring, so it never ran dry. I scooped some with my hand and brought it to my lips to drink.

"Deborah."

I turned toward the sound. "I am here."

"I have been waiting for you." My love's voice was a warm and welcoming presence that promised laughter and happiness.

I could not see him, but he liked to tease me by hiding. "Where are you?" I left the fountain and began to search for him, smiling as I went. Any moment now, he might jump out and catch me in his arms and whirl me about. "Come out, beloved."

"Deborah." His voice changed. "Deborah, I cannot see you."

The bright sunlight had faded a little, and I looked up to see the sky turning dark with storm clouds. It would rain soon.

"I am here." I pushed aside a tangle of vines. "Come to me, and we will go back into the house." If I could find the way to the house. It had grown so dark, I could not see the path leading out of the garden anymore.

"I cannot find you." He sounded anxious. "Deborah, hurry."

Lightning slashed across the black clouds, and wind rushed through the garden to tear at my clothes. I threw up my hands as leaves pelted my face. "I must leave you now. Take shelter."

"Deborah, do not go!"

I turned this way and that, trying to avoid being lashed by the waving branches of the trees. Flowers flew away on the wind, torn from their stems. The light was gone, the sun swallowed by the storm, and I reached out my hand to feel my way.

A hole appeared a few feet away from me on the ground, jagged-edged and black as pitch.

A sharp pain struck my shoulder, and I cried out as I fell. I did not want to leave the garden, for it was the only place I felt safe, but I would die if I stayed. "Farewell," I sobbed, crawling toward the ugly scar in the earth. "Farewell, my love."

"Deborah, come back! I shall get you to safety! I shall get—"

Get.

Get up.

"Do your ears not work?" Something slammed into my shoulder again. "Get up, you lazy slut."

The hard kick knocked me forward, so that I lay facedown in the straw. I bit back another cry and quickly curled over, pushing myself up onto my knees.

Ybyon stood over me, his broad face a mask of ugly shadows, his eyes narrow with contempt. "On your feet, girl."

The corner of the barn where I slept was silent, and only the light from the hanging lamp the master carried illuminated the darkness. The others who slumbered next to me in the straw were already gone; I had slept too long again.

"Forgive me, Adon," I begged as I stood and tugged my middo down over my thighs. It hung loosely, for it had once belonged to one of the kitchen wenches. I was given it when it became too stained and threadbare for her to wear. That it was too large did not matter to me. It covered my body and gave me a little warmth at night when I slept.

Ybyon paused, as if deciding whether to kick me again. "Get to work." He turned and stalked out to the pens.

Because it was so near dawn, I did not dare leave the barn and go to the kitchens for my bread. Instead I retrieved my pan from where it hung on the wall and carried it to the first stall. The old, bad-tempered spotted goat kept there was eating a pile of scraps from the kitchen refuse heap, and she bleated her annoyance as I crouched beside her.

I said nothing when she butted my aching shoulder. I milked her quickly and whisked the pan from beneath her before she could kick it over with her hooves. Her milk warmed the pan and floated, thick and foamy around the edges. I looked from side to side and then bent my head to drink a mouthful before I carried the pan out of the stall.

"Deborah." Meji came and took the pan from me, and he looked about before saying in a whisper, "Sorry. I tried to wake you, but you would not move, and then Hlagor shouted for me."

"It matters not." That I had slept too long on a morning when I knew Ybyon would come to inspect the barns and stables was my fault. I had sat up alone last night, watching stars shoot across the sky, when I should have been sleeping. I heard the master's voice drawing close and touched Meji's thin arm before I hurried out to the pens.

Ybyon owned five hundred sheep and two

hundred goats, as well as some cows, mules, oxen, and onagers. One of his businesses was the buying and selling of beasts, so the number occupying the pens and stalls constantly changed. My morning task was to check the sheep pens and see that no lambs had been dropped or injured during the night. In winter I hated going into the pens, for I always found too many of the early births had expired from the cold or been trampled to death. Now that it was almost spring, I would have to be more vigilant; the fat ewes would begin dropping their lambs by the dozen each night.

The sheep pen smelled much worse than the barn, and the ground beneath my bare feet was slick with manure. Many of the sheep needed their hooves cut back and cleaned out, for they had grown over, but that would not be done until they were sold. Their wool was thick and greasy to the touch, and their dark narrow heads turned to look at me as I waded through them.

I saw one of the ewes by the fence, standing as far from the herd as she could manage in the confines of the pen. A stringy, wet mass was hanging from beneath her chubby tail, the afterbirth that spilled from her after dropping the lamb that lay curled on the ground beneath her.

The lamb was at suck, and the ewe lowered her head as I approached, but I did not disturb them. If I tried to take the lamb now, the ewe would charge me. Instead I watched the little one have his first meal. I had never known my own mother, so such things drew me.

"Girl!" Ybyon strode toward me, driving the sheep out of his way. "Why do you idle there?"

I bowed my head. "It is a new lamb, Adon."

"Yes, yes, I can see that." He clouted the side of my head with his fist. "Why do you not carry it to the lamb pen?"

I cringed and pressed my fingers to my throbbing ear. "It is nursing, Adon."

Ybyon reached down, tore the lamb from its mother, and shoved it into my arms. "Now it is not. Take it."

The ewe reacted strongly to this intrusion by charging Ybyon. The master caught her by the neck and spun her around, flinging her into the fence. She lay there, stunned and unmoving.

"If she does not rise to go to graze, have one of the shepherds cut her throat," Ybyon told me before he stalked out of the pen.

"Yes, Adon." I cuddled the bleating lamb close to my chest. I did not dare take him back to his mother to try to rouse her. I never disobeyed Ybyon or questioned what he wished done with his property. No matter how cruel or unfair his orders were, I always carried them out.

I did this because I, too, was Ybyon's property—his slave, from the moment of my birth, just as my mother had been. If I did not do exactly what my master said, he would not send for one of the shepherds to cut my throat.

He would do it himself. As he had when he killed my mother.

By the time I returned from carrying the struggling, bleating lamb to the newborn pen, the ewe had risen from the mud. Now she nosed her way through the flock as she baaed, wide-eyed and frantic, for the lamb I had taken from her. I saw under her tail the bulge of the watery sac that had held the lamb inside her, and saw it drop onto the cold muddy ground. Quickly I picked up the sac and ran with it back to the lamb pen, where I rubbed it all over the newborn, soaking its wool with the fluid, especially its bottom end.

A shepherd had taught me the trick; if the lamb was permitted to rejoin the herd, the ewe would recognize him by the smell.

I shut my ears to the sound of the lamb's loud calls for his mother, and looked away from the confusion and fear in his small dark eyes. I had done all I could for him; the rest would be the master's say. The newborn might rejoin the herd, or he might end up a fancy dish on a rich man's table. The master did not keep many rams.

Most of the animals Ybyon kept were fattened and sold at market, many purchased by other rich men in Hazor for their meat. The best were butchered to feed Ybyon's family, for greatly beloved as they were by my master, they ate meat every week.

"She is strong," Meji said as he came to walk back to the main herd pen beside me. "A good breeder, too. The lamb will thrive."

"Not if he cannot suck." The first days of feeding were the most important, too, for the ewe's milk was especially thick and rich with something that helped its lamb grow large and strong. Too many times I had seen a nervous ewe that had never birthed before reject its lamb without allowing it to suck. Even when fed with a milk-soaked rag, the little one almost always died. "Why did the master not let her stay behind?"

"Why does the master do anything? Because he wishes to." Meji's worn, dirty middo was covered with bits of dried grass from the bale of new green grass shoots he carried to the lamb pen. He nudged me with a bony elbow, and held out something to me. "Here, Deborah. To keep *you* strong."

I did not feel very strong, not when he tucked a slightly squashed wedge of white goat's-milk cheese into my hand. "Meji." I had not tasted cheese in months, and quickly closed my fingers over it. "I am more grateful than I can say, but if Seres ever catches you stealing from the kitchen—"

"I did not steal it—I promise you." Meji grinned before he carried the bale away from the hungry mouths of the sheep and into the barn.

I looked around carefully before I lifted my hand as if to cover a cough and took a secret bite of the cheese. Newly ripe, it tasted fresh and soft and made my mouth water. It was hard not to gobble up the rest, but my stomach felt so empty that I feared I would retch if I did. I lowered my hand, tucking the rest of the wedge in the rolled edge of my sleeve before I walked after Meji.

The flock would be kept outside until the shepherds came with their dogs to herd them down the hill. There, in the green pastures by the river, the sheep would graze and nap in the sweet grass until the sun began to sink into the western skies, when the shepherds would drive them back up the hill to the farm.

What would it be like, I wondered as I looked out at the valley beneath the city, to spend the whole day doing nothing but eating and sleeping? Far in the distance, I could see the shimmering blue of Lake Huleh. I had never left Hazor, but I often daydreamed of walking across the valley to the lake and bathing in those cool waters.

I wonder if there are flowers there, I thought, recalling my dream of the beautiful garden. *And that man who searches for me—*

"You, girl." Hlagor, the master's stable-man, scowled at me as he walked past with a sack of grain balanced on his shoulder. "Stop standing about, and get to work."

CHAPTER 2

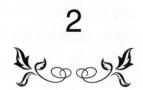

I hurried back to the barn. My next task was to use a rake to clean out the soiled straw from every stall and pen, pile it in the muck cart, and haul it to the dung heap. It was filthy, odorous work, with flies buzzing all around me, but it had to be done or the animals would become footsore. While I raked up the urine- and manure-stained straw, I also had to kill any vermin I found. It was another burden I disliked, but my master had a particular and intense loathing for rats, and he would beat me without mercy if he saw or heard any in the barns.

As soon as I cleaned out one area, Meji

and some of the other young men would carry in sheaves of fresh dried straw to spread over the muddy floor. The clean bedding kept the animals from developing sores on their hooves and bodies, and it lightened the ever-present odor of dung from the barn.

Hlagor kept a sharp eye on all of us as he made his rounds, filling the clean feed troughs with grain. He was short and thick-bodied, and kept the wiry black hair on his skull and face cropped close to the skin. Although he was slave-born like the rest of us, Hlagor held the position of a free man. Ybyon treated him differently, too—almost as if he were paid instead of owned.

As long as they worked hard, Hlagor treated Meji and the other men well enough. The stableman didn't like me, however, and he did not know of my gift. More than once he had given me the back of his hand for little reason.

"He was the same with your mother," Meji told me once during the cold season, when we lay huddled together in the straw to share our warmth. "She refused him, and it soured his heart against her and you."

"Refused him?" I drew back as Meji made a crude gesture with his fingers, imitating the motions of a ram mounting a ewe. "No one told me that my mother served in the house." She had been a stable slave, the same as I. Then I thought of the other way a woman could be made to serve.

Women used to give relief to Ybyon's hands were kept in the back section of the main farmhouse, where the master's hired men slept. When the women were not attending to men's needs, they were put to work by the housekeeper, washing and bundling shorn fleeces for market. Despite this, their lives were far more comfortable than mine or my mother's had been.

Meji pressed my cold, thin fingers between his own strong, bony hands. "It was said that your mother served the master himself," he whispered. "That is why Hlagor desired her."

I had been a slave all my life, so I understood how men used women to relieve their needs. It was as much a part of life on the farm as when the rams were brought to breed the ewes, and often just as indiscreet. Still, I could not imagine my mother serving Ybyon any more than I could her giving relief to Hlagor. My mother had not been a pretty woman, according to the shepherds who spoke of her. Her face had been branded across the brow with a witch mark, and she had borne many other scars, most likely inflicted by Ybyon's frequent beatings. The other slaves had deferred to her because of her gift, but none desired her. In truth, most admitted that they had feared her touch.

Had the master known of my mother's gift? I would have asked Meji, but by that time he had fallen asleep. He seemed to regret saying as much as he had to me, for every time after that, he avoided my questions about my mother, Ybyon, and Hlagor, and we never discussed the matter again.

My arms and back were aching by the time I had finished mucking out one side of the barn, and as soon as I saw Hlagor walk up to the main house for the midday meal, I slipped out to use the privy. On the walk down the path, I risked taking another bite of the cheese Meji had stolen for me. The second taste was more delicious than the first.

If I had not been slave-born, I might have married a wealthy trader who would buy me cheese to eat every day. My eyelids drooped as I imagined the bounty of food to be had as a free woman. The master bought huge wheels of cheese for his family, and kept bowls heaped with ripe brown dates on the tables. His children drank five full jugs of goat's milk every day, and they gobbled up countless loaves of golden lehem made from smooth, sifted qemah. I knew this because when I was younger I would watch them eat, spying through the window slits at the back of the kitchen. Now and then the old cook would notice me, and being blessed with a soft heart, she would sometimes give me a handful of scraps from the master's table.

I tucked the morsel of cheese back into my sleeve, saving the last bit for later, and blinked hard. I was tired of being so hungry that all I thought of was food I would never eat, and freedom I would never enjoy.

Offer thanks to the One God for what you have, my mother would tell me in my dreams, *not complaints about what you do not. His favor is shown not to those who ask, but to those who ask not.*

I had never asked Jehovah for anything, but He had not blessed me with His favor, so I did not know if her words were true. That I dreamed of a mother I could not remember made me wonder if in my loneliness I was not imagining it all.

The slaves' privy was only a pit covered by wooden planks, but at least this one was not out in the open. When the old pit had been filled, the men had dug the new one between three old terebinth trees. The oaks' wide, gnarled trunks provided a little privacy for the female slaves, who were obliged to lift their skirts, crouch, and perch unsteadily over the plank holes. The resins collected from slashes in the trees' bark, which the men used in many ways, also left a sharp, cleansing odor that chased away the smell of the pit.

I had just finished making my water when I heard footsteps shuffling through dry grass beyond the trees, and the master's voice speaking.

"It is a long journey from Ephraim to Hazor," he said, in the fawning manner he used with the wealthy men who sometimes came to inspect the flocks. "Did you not first try the markets at Taanach or Megiddo?"

I nearly tumbled over when I heard the reply. "The southern Canaanite kings have decreed that no merchant in Ephraim may sell livestock to anyone but the supply caravans for their armies. We are obliged to travel far north now to supplement our herds."

The merchant's low, pleasant voice was strangely accented, but I knew it, for I had heard it before, many times—calling to me in my dreams.

I pulled down the frayed hem of my middo and moved between the trunks of the two largest trees, wedging myself there, where I could observe but would not be seen. I spied on my master as he walked slowly across the pasture with the merchant whose voice I knew as well as my own.

The merchant was not one of the many who came to barter with Ybyon for livestock and wool. This man's kesut was long and simply fashioned, as was his head covering, not at all like the merchants of Hazor, who dressed in grand, richly ornamented garb. Also, his clothing had been fashioned from thick, dense wool, as if the man had dressed expecting cold weather. A short, sun-lightened brown beard covered the lower half of his face, but it was trimmed, not oiled or braided. The corners of his long dark eyes were tilted, the lids darkened with green-black kohl.

Who was this man? I had never seen any-one like him, but there was something about him that seemed familiar—as if I should have known him.

I shifted around the trunk to move out of the sunlight and get a better look. Quite handsome, this merchant was, but perhaps what caught my eye was the lack of adornments. I thought some of the master's buyers looked more like women than men, so bejeweled and perfumed were they. His ears and nostrils were not pierced, as was also common among the men of Hazor, and no tattoos or brands proclaiming his patron god marred his tanned brow. The finely worked copper chain around his neck sported no protective pendant or talisman against curses. He was also unusually tall, one of the tallest men I had ever seen, and he moved in such a way as to make my master appear squat and ungainly.

"I shall need one hundred healthy young ewes and thirty fertile rams," the merchant was saying to Ybyon. "You may deliver them to the river crossing the morning after Sabbath."

Sabbath. I covered my mouth with my hand to smother the groan that rose in my throat. No wonder he had no god-symbols or talismans: he was a Hebrew. A stupid one, at that, for he did not know how much Ybyon loathed our people. Why would he reveal himself so openly? He was alone, with no personal guards or retainers to defend him. Did he not know that Hazor had no treaty with Israel, and the Canaanites here despised our kind so much they would happily hang him from the king's gatepost to feed the vultures?

My master paused and stared at him for a long moment. "You are a Hebrew, Merchant Lappidoth?"

Lappidoth. The name seized me like an angry hand, making me forget everything else, even the helpless terror of knowing a man was about to die a painful, undeserved death.

"I am, but my father was Lappidoth," the foolish man replied. "I bear his name, but Jeth is how I am called."

Many young Hebrew men named after their sires were given different family names to avoid confusion, but that was not what seized my heart with new dread.

When I was very young, my mother came into my dreams and spoke of this man. She had known his surname, Lappidoth, and had described him to me. He looked familiar because he appeared exactly as the woman in my dreams had said.

Someday this man's life will cross yours, Deborah, Dasah had said. *Do not avoid him, or it will mean death for both of you.*

As a child I had not understood the disturbing dream portent any more than I did now. The message upset me, though, and I had much trouble sleeping for weeks after one of the dreams. I had many bad dreams, dreams of great battles and men falling around me and blood staining the land, but I tried to forget them as soon as I woke. Now here was the man from the dream of my mother, exactly as she had described him, bearing the name she had repeated over and over, so that I would never forget.

Jeth Lappidoth, the man my dream mother had predicted would come, was here now crossing my life. Would he bring sorrow and misery to me? Who would not avoid such a man?

"I thought you were of the Rephaim," Ybyon was saying.

"You did?" Jeth sounded a little amused. "The Rephaim are cowards and outlaws, who hide in our mountains and prey on unprotected travelers." His gaze moved over

Ybyon's features. "I worship Jehovah, but my silver is no different from any Canaanite's."

I covered my eyes, for by saying such a thing, his fate had been sealed, and now Death would come for him. No Canaanite would tolerate being compared to a Hebrew, least of all Ybyon. At any moment, my master would strike down the foolish son of Israel and kick him until his blood turned the grass crimson and his bones were dust.

"As you say," I heard Ybyon reply in a calm, unperturbed tone. "Yes, I can deliver one hundred and thirty in three days to the river crossing."

"I shall have payment waiting for you," Jeth promised.

I looked through my fingers to see the two men clasping hands, the way men did after coming to a business agreement. My master was smiling with pleasure at this Hebrew merchant, as if they were on the friendliest of terms. There would be no beating, no killing.

That was not possible, unless my master had suddenly gone completely mad.

I waited until they walked out of sight before I ran to the barn. Hlagor was still up at the main house, likely meddling with one of the kitchen slaves, as he used them often. I hoped he would take his time, for there was still half the work waiting for me to finish. I would have to do it quickly before his return, or the stableman would take a switch to my back.

I went to the next stall to be cleaned out, only to find the work done. The others were the same, and when I checked the barrow, it was empty. Someone had done my work for me, and even carted the soiled grass out to the refuse heap.

"There you are," a relieved voice said behind me. "We thought you had run away."

I turned around to see Meji and two of the younger men standing behind me. They held sheaves of fresh, clean straw to spread, and dirt from the work that I should have done stained their hands and arms.

"You should not have done this," I scolded him, keeping my voice low. "Do you not have enough tasks of your own to do?"

"We grew restless waiting for you to return." Meji thrust a sheaf into my arms. "If you feel so guilty, you may help us."

Together we worked until the floor of the barn was covered with fresh bedding. The men liked to talk and jest with each other, but they were silent around me. I did not mind the quiet—my thoughts were filled with the Hebrew merchant I had seen with Ybyon.

Jeth Lappidoth. How had my dream mother known his surname? Was it so common, or was the man some kin to her? Had he promised to come for her? Had she known that he would come to Hazor someday?

More puzzling was what I had witnessed. Why had the master been so amiable toward Jeth? That Ybyon hated Hebrews was well known, even among his slaves. Often we heard him speak fondly of his grandparents, who had traveled to Hazor from Jericho just before the Hebrews had come out of the wilderness to invade Canaan. Jericho had been the first city the Hebrew general Joshua had destroyed. Ybyon's grandparents lost every member of their family in the battle. They could not return, either, for after the Hebrews had brought down the mighty walls of Jericho, they had burned the city to the ground.

"Hebrews are like rats," Ybyon would often say. "Let one go free, and in a week you have forty more gnawing at your sandal straps."

That was one of the kinder remarks my master made. There were other, far worse things that came from his mouth that I tried not to hear.

I knew a little of the politics involved in the Hebrews coming to Canaan from listening to the master and some of his older shepherds talk about it. Egypt had enslaved my people for centuries, until Jehovah had brought so many plagues that Pharaoh had freed the Hebrews and sent them into the wilderness. There they wandered for many years, punished by the One God for their own sins, until such time as they were cleansed and prepared to enter the Promised Land. So they did, as an army of nomad tribes, hardened by years of struggle and loss. They conquered everything in their path, and killed those who stood in their way.

How my mother became separated from her tribe, I knew not. She had never spoken of them or her life before she had been sold into slavery, but I always suspected it was something more terrible than she wished anyone to know.

Then, too, the older slaves who had known Dasah were always reluctant to speak of her.

"The past is a grave, Deborah," Tarn, the oldest slave among us, told me whenever I asked about her. "Do not dig it up from the ground, for you will not like what comes out of the dirt."

Over time some of the Canaanites had accepted the presence of Hebrews in their land, and had struck treaties with the armies to protect their cities from attack. King Jabin of Hazor was not one of these, and he had sent his armies to attack many Hebrew settlements. Thanks to our king, the Canaanites of Hazor would not acknowledge our faith or worshipping the One God, and they ridiculed our belief in His promise that this land would be ours. Some did worse; I had long suspected that the master bought mostly Hebrew slaves to take pleasure in overworking and abusing us. Perhaps he thought it proper revenge for what Joshua and his armies had done to his family.

"Outside with all of you," Hlagor called from the open door of the barn. We filed past him and into the bright sunlight, where we waited while he inspected the work we had done. He came out looking more disgruntled than ever, and passed me without a glance.

"High praise," Meji whispered. "Soon he

will be so overcome with joy of us that he will make his mark on our freedom scrolls."

"Of course he will," I murmured. "Just as soon as the stars fall to earth and the sheep shear themselves."

"You must tell me if you dream of that," my friend murmured, and grinned. "I will take a bucket and catch a star for you."

CHAPTER
3

As soon as the stableman stalked out of sight, two kitchen servants carried a large pot, a basket, and several rounds of rough brown lehem, which they handed to Tarn for our midday meal.

Tarn was so old that all his hair had turned silver. Like me, he had been enslaved since birth, but most of his life had been spent serving a trader whose caravans crossed the length and breadth of Canaan. The deep, old scar across the front of his throat bespoke of his strength and endurance. When I was a little girl, he had told me how he received it as a punishment for trying to run away from his master. He had been caught, brought back, and tied to the back of a mule with a slip-knotted rope around his neck. He had been forced to walk thus for the three weeks it took his master's caravan to cross the southern desert, and several times had fallen and nearly choked to death.

"When you look at me," he warned, "remember that every time a slave defies his master, he risks his neck."

The pot and bread were carried to the shady side of the barn, where the men sat in a circle as I divided the bread among us. We dipped our pieces into the pot to soak up the thin bean porridge inside, made of water and twice-cooked adasim and himmesim, but as always there was only half a pot, so it was soon emptied. The basket held a meager amount of overripe siqma figs, which I also portioned out to the men.

"That is all?" Chemesh, one of the newer slaves, complained as I handed him his share.

"I am sorry." I felt guilty, although I had no say over how much food we were given. None of us did. "This is all that was brought today."

Chemesh's face darkened. "Why do you decide what I eat? You are only a woman."

Some of the men looked at each other. No one looked at me. New slaves were not told of my gift until we could rely on them to hold their tongues and follow our ways. Chemesh had been brought to the farm only two weeks past; no one trusted him.

"Serving food is a woman's task," Tarn, the eldest of the stable slaves, said. "Deborah is honest and fair to all." He glanced at the two withered figs that I had taken for my portion. "Except to herself." To me, he said, "You should have more than that, girl. You missed the morning meal."

I smiled at him. "My stomach will wake me earlier tomorrow."

I did give the men more food than I took for myself, but that was only right, for they were bigger, did heavier work, and needed more food. It hurt me to know how hungry they were, for the master's stinginess showed in the gauntness of their bodies and the hollows in their faces. I was fortunate to have had the cheese Meji had given me—without it I would have spent the rest of the day feeling dizzy and strange-headed.

"I am starving here," Chemesh muttered.

"Has anyone more?" As the other men shook their heads, he hit the ground with his fist. "A babe could not be sustained on what we are given."

Tarn shrugged. "Eat less, sleep light, and work more."

"We cannot work at all," Chemesh said, "if we are reduced to sticks. Can you not speak to Hlagor, and tell him we need more than this?"

Tarn, who had been shearing sheep for the master since he was a boy, squinted at the younger man. "Balaa, the man whose place you take in this circle, also did not think we were given enough to eat, and he spoke of this and other grievances to Hlagor. The next day the master lashed Balaa to the counting post in the fleece shed and whipped him, then left him there to bleed. It took him three days to die."

I glanced at the shed, which stood across the field, away from the barn, and shuddered at the memory Tarn's warning had brought back. I had wept and cringed, hearing poor Balaa's screams as the master had beaten him, and then later, his weak cries for mercy. But no one had been permitted to help him, for Ybyon had chained guard dogs to the door of the shed, and they barked at anyone who had approached.

"Every word said to Hlagor is heard by the master's ears," Meji said, and grimaced. "If your belly pains you, eat a handful of grain. That will fill in the holes as well as qali."

"Eat uncooked fodder from the animal troughs?" Chemesh sounded revolted. "I am not a sheep."

"Let the master or the stableman catch you eating grain or any stolen food," Tarn said, looking from the new slave to Meji and me, "and they will chop you up and feed you to the dogs."

Meji went on eating, wholly unconcerned. I suppressed a shudder. Tarn might be old, but he had sharp eyes for misbehavior among our ranks.

We did not linger; as soon as the last food had been eaten, the men rose and went back to work. Another of my daily tasks was to carry the empty pot and basket back up to the main house. I disliked this chore even more than cleaning the matted plugs of waste from under the chubby tails of the sheep, because the kitchen slaves were considered superior to those of us who worked out on the farm. Most of them ignored me, but there were a few who took pleasure in finding ways to taunt and torment me.

I tried to slip into the kitchen without attracting notice. The slaves who worked preparing food were constantly busy, for Ybyon's family numbered twenty-nine, including his grandparents, his parents, a wife and her widowed mother, his three sons, five daughters, their wives and husbands, and seven grandchildren. Although the master's sons and daughters lived in their own small pillared houses next to the master's, the entire family gathered twice daily in the main house for their meals.

Ybyon did not begrudge his own kin food, and the meals prepared for them were very grand: cooked stews of kid and pol, flavored with spices and onions and thickened with hitta; qali soaked in broth until the grains burst and became a mush, to which honey and sesame were added; lehem made from the finest hitta; cakes of tahan-rolled dates; zetim pickled in brine, pitted and stuffed with pistachio nuts; whole roasted haunches of mutton studded with cloves of garlic; and wild fowl baked in wine with whole eggs from their own nests. Then came the sweetmeats, honeyed pistachios, figs laced with fruit syrups, and cakes of every size and variety, from grainy ugot with raisins to delicate emmer crisps dotted with flecks of cinnamon and tiny currants.

The food was another reason I disliked going to the kitchen so much: it was forbidden for slaves to touch a crumb of the delicious foods prepared for the master's table. My perpetual hunger made seeing and smelling the contents of the heavily laden bowls and platters as much an ordeal as mucking out the stable.

To resist temptation, I never lingered, but that did not always work. As it did not on this day.

"Stable girl," one of the wenches called out as I tried to slip into the kitchen unnoticed. It was the big wench whose old middo I had inherited. She was forever making dove eyes at Meji, who would not give her a second glance. "Come here."

I placed the pot and basket where Seres, the master's present cook, desired them, and walked slowly over to where the older women were preparing meat for the master's grand meal of the evening.

A young goat's carcass had already been

spitted and was being slowly turned over the heat from glowing white-edged scarlet coals. Most of the fat was saved and coated the meat with each turn of the spit, but a few drops fell to sizzle on the coals, and lent a delicious, smoky scent to the air.

Meat, something slaves were never fed, was a particular torment.

My stomach twisted into a knot as I crouched on my haunches in front of the female who had called to me. She was one of the younger females purchased by the master to serve in the house. She was not pretty, only ordinary-looking, but the One and True God had blessed her with an ample bosom and broad hips, which swayed with enticing movements whenever she walked. Often I saw her jiggling herself in front of Meji, so much so at times that I thought she might do herself an injury.

"Stable girl," she repeated, although she and every other female working in the house knew well my name, "hand me that bowl there."

I followed the gesture she made and saw a huge block of honeycomb oozing golden sweetness into a shallow wooden bowl. I had tasted honey only once or twice before, spread on cakes that the old cook had given me as a special treat. Carefully I picked up the bowl and brought it to her, and watched as she poured a measure of honey into the sauce she was mixing. Then she ran the tips of three of her fingers over the comb, and lifted them dripping with honey to her lips, where she licked and sucked each one clean.

"Mmmmmm. You would like some of this, wouldn't you, stable girl?" the wench asked as she moved the bowl toward me, as if offering it.

I knew her game, for she played it often. If I said yes, she would laugh and take the bowl away. If I said no, she would laugh and call me a liar and still take the bowl away. So I kept my eyes on the oiled dirt floor, said nothing, and hoped she would quickly tire of taunting me. In my mind's eye, I saw a flash of two images—a foot drawn back to kick, and honey spilling on dirt. Such things often popped into my head just before they happened.

"Do you know, it is so sweet"—a honey-coated finger wagged under my nose—"that it makes your teeth ache?"

"Wasi." A big, grease-smeared fist boxed

the girl on the side of the head, so quick and hard, she nearly fell into the cooking pit. "Get that sauce made and baste the meat proper ere I take a switch to your ass."

I stayed where I was, for I feared Seres almost as much as I did the master.

"You."

Knowing he was speaking now to me, I looked up into the kitchen steward's angry eyes. Seres was an enormous man, his bulk easily that of three men put together. His head was bald, and his face clean-shaven, but the rest of him was quite black with hair. Odd tufts sprouted from his nostrils and ears, and grew down his neck to cover his back in long, wiry patches. He was one of the few slaves Ybyon owned who was not a Hebrew, but a Libyan. He had been brought to the farm to replace the old cook when she had died, but had instantly taken over the kitchen and all who toiled in it, and ran it like a slave master. No one had yet dared to call him Cook; to all, he was the kitchen steward.

"What do you here?" he demanded.

I bowed my head a little lower. "I return the pot and basket, Zaqen."

"She crept over here to steal from the

master's table," the kitchen wench sniveled. "I stopped her."

"Steal that which you near rubbed in her face?" Seres clouted the wench a second time, and she huddled, weeping as she covered her head with her hands. He then glared at me. "Get you back to the stable, girl, before someone sees you gone."

I nodded and rose to hurry away, but as the big man turned, he drew back his foot to kick the wench. I saw that one of his feet would collide with the bowl of honey, which remained where the wench had dropped it. My tormentor dropped her hands and screeched as she saw the same, but she covered her face instead of reaching for the bowl.

Seres did not see the bowl at all.

The thought of wasting such a precious thing made me react. A moment after Seres's foot knocked into the bowl and flipped it over onto its side, I crouched down and caught it with my left hand.

"No!" the wench shrieked. "Don't touch it! Your hand is filthy!"

I was left-handed, something that made the superstitious slaves uneasy, for it was custom to use the left hand at the privy and the right hand for eating and everything else. I could not help that I had reached with my left hand, but I was careful not to touch the contents as I lifted and offered the bowl of honey to Seres.

He took it and gave me a sharp look. "You are the daughter of Dasah, are you not?" I nodded. "What do you here, girl?"

"I brought back the master's vessels from the stable." Was he angry? Did he mean to punish me for laying hands on the master's food? His fists were so big that my shoulders wanted to shrivel.

"You are very quick, Deborah, even if you do not use the right hand." He nodded as if to himself, and then made a terse gesture. "Go, return to your work."

CHAPTER
4

I wanted to return to the warmth of the kitchens the moment I left them, for thick dark clouds covered the sun, and the midwinter wind had risen, hard and biting cold. But from the shadows cast on the ground, I knew the shepherds would return soon. The goats and ewes would need to be milked, and the early lambs brought to suck, and a thousand other tasks waited to be finished before sunset. We would have nothing else to eat this day. Perhaps it was as Tarn said, and the master believed we would sleep less and work more if we went to bed hungry.

No, I told myself, thinking of the thin bodies of the other stable slaves. Ybyon knew how to keep his animals plump and in good health; there was no reason he would not do the same with his slaves unless . . . *Does he starve us for his pleasure?*

To add to my misery, a silver torrent of hard rain swept over me before I could reach the barn, soaking me through. When I felt the sting of ice against my arms, I covered my face with my hands to protect my eyes. Larger frozen balls struck my scalp and shoulders. A few steps from the closed barn door, I ran into something almost as large and hard as a massebot—only this standing stone had arms that pulled me away from the door and wrapped me in smothering cloth.

"Hold still, boy," a familiar voice said as hands adjusted the cloth to uncover my face. "I mean you no harm."

At last I could see, but I was nearly pressed against the plain wool of a kesut. I looked up into kindly brown eyes, the centers of which were flecked with light green specks. It was the Hebrew merchant, Lappidoth, and he had pulled me under one of the corner eaves, behind a stack of rough-hewn wood planks used to repair the pens.

"No, wait here," he said, placing his hands on my shoulders, holding me when I would have darted away. He had large, strong hands, the palms and insides of the fingers callused. No pampered merchant of Hazor had such hands. "The hail is too thick. It will crack your head open."

I eased from under his touch. The sound of the hail striking the barn roof and trees was so loud, it hurt my ears, and I had to speak loudly to be heard. "I must go inside and see to the animals, Adon."

"They can wait, as well, boy—and my name is Jeth."

Knowing his given name made me more uneasy. I could not call him by that or any title but Adon. This close, I could smell the strange spices scenting his kesut, and feel the warmth of his strong, gentle hands as it burned through the shabby yoke of my middo. He had to be the cleanest person I had ever seen in my life; his teeth, his skin—even his hair gleamed with care and good health.

The next instant I realized how filthy I must seem to him; my face sweaty from hurrying down to the barn, and my ragged, castoff middo smelling of sheep and manure. My own hair I kept as clean as I could, pulled back from my face in a rough braid tied at the end with a bit of twine, but I had nothing but my fingers with which to comb it, so even braided it was a mass of tangles.

I bit my lip and tried to edge away, but he caught my arms. "I must go." I squirmed out of his hands. "I am needed."

"When the hail began, I tried to go in there myself, but the door is bolted from the inside." He gave me an encouraging smile. "I will not harm you, boy."

Did I look so boyish, then? Why was he lurking about the barn? "What do you here, Adon?"

"I came to buy sheep. My mule is stabled inside with the others." He sighed and gazed out at the horizon. "I hope the storm passes soon. I must return to my rooms before sunset, or the innkeeper, Dhiban, will rent them over to another for the night."

"Is it so crowded in town?" We were never permitted to leave the farm, and so I had seen little of my birthplace.

He nodded. "Many merchants have come up from the southern lands, looking for livestock to replenish their herds. Ephraim's markets belong to the armies now." He gazed down at me, his expression growing puzzled as he picked up my long braid with his hand. "Now I see that you are not a boy, or a child. What is your name?"

I wanted to lie to him, afraid that he had known my mother or had been one of those who had sinned against her, but my tongue would not cooperate. "I am called Deborah, Adon."

There was no recognition in his eyes. "That is a Hebrew name."

I nodded. "My mother was said to be Hebrew." No one would speak of who my father had been, save to tell me that he was not a Hebrew. I guessed that he must have been one of the shepherds. Tarn had told me that my mother had been enslaved since childhood, and while she never spoke of her people, that it was likely that her own tribe had sold her or cast her out.

Jeth seemed startled by my admission. "I should have guessed as much from your coloring and the shape of your eyes." He glanced down at my middo, and his mouth became a hard, straight line. "How does a daughter of Jehovah come to be living here, among the Canaanites? Did your mother wed outside the tribe?"

I had to swallow a bitter laugh. Did he not see the rags I wore? Did he think a daughter of the house would work in the barn?

"My mother was not wed, Adon. She was a slave." I pulled up my sleeve and showed him the scar left by Ybyon's branding iron on the inside of my forearm. "I am slave-born. I belong to Adon Ybyon."

A small line appeared between Jeth's smooth dark brows, and he put out his hand and traced the shiny lines of my scar. "How can this be? Who could have—"

"Deborah." Meji appeared, and his face paled when he saw me standing beside Lappidoth. "Hlagor comes."

I nodded and looked up at my savior and tormentor. "I am needed in the barn. Safe journey, Adon." Before he could speak again, I went with Meji into the side door of the barn.

"Here." Meji tugged me into one of the stalls and took me by the arms to turn me while he looked all over me. "You were caught in the hail."

"Almost. That wench who forever ogles you had to taunt me." I tried not to think about the honey I hadn't tasted. "The storm came before I could reach the barn, but the merchant helped me."

"Merchants." He spat on the floor before renewing his inspection. "They care only for silver. What else did he do to you?"

"He protected me from the hail. We spoke a little." Why was Meji behaving like this? "Jeth is a Hebrew, from Ephraim. A good man, I think." My friend seemed deaf to my assurances. "Meji, he did nothing to harm me."

"He had his hands on you. Maybe he did not have time enough to do more." He parted my hair to inspect my scalp, then seemed satisfied that I had no injuries. He rested his hands against my cheeks briefly. "If the master had seen you near him . . . No, I do not wish to imagine that. You cannot speak to that man again."

I felt a strange pain in my breast as I remembered the kindness in Jeth's warm eyes. "I do not think I will *see* that man again."

The shepherds came late with the flocks, as the storm had forced them to drive the herd into a grove of trees and keep them there while the branches provided a little protection against the hailstorm. Many of the flock had still received small injuries to their heads and backs, which we tended, and all the animals were tired and distressed. Some of the men had bumps and bruises from being struck by the hail, as well.

"It is an evil omen," one of the older shepherds claimed as Meji washed a bloody wound on his head. "Jehovah weeps tears of anger, and hurls them at those who have wounded His heart."

"It is rain that froze while it was in the clouds, seba," Meji said. "It comes often enough, no matter what Jehovah's mood is."

I brought a poultice of mashed grain, water, and a little of the yellow powder the shepherds used on the sheep when their feet festered, and gave Meji a length of rag to use to bind the wound. "Jehovah has no reason to be displeased with us. We are faithful to Him."

"We do not keep the Sabbath," the old one argued. "We live under the yoke. Our master is a—"

"Good, fair man who indulges us too often," Tarn said suddenly, and very loudly. "As Adon Hlagor has told us, many times."

The old shepherd glared at Tarn, and then saw the steward walk in and fell silent. From Hlagor's gloating expression, he had been standing outside eavesdropping on us, and had heard every word said.

"So, Eban, you think your One pitiful God is angry with you?" He gazed around at the wounded animals. "Wait until the master hears of how poorly you have tended his flock, and how much you have complained. More things will be bruised than your head."

Chemesh muttered something ugly under his breath.

Hlagor heard and pointed to the new slave. "You, there. Brave one. Come here and say that again where I can hear it."

I saw Chemesh pick up a length of wood as he rose to his feet, and tuck it out of sight behind his leg. In my mind I saw him charging at Hlagor, shouting and clubbing him over the head. If Chemesh killed the steward, Ybyon would have him tortured to death.

"Adon Hlagor," I said, stepping between him and Chemesh to block his view. I had to get him out of here. "I must tell you of a strange man who was here, just outside the barn, when the storm came." I remembered that I was not supposed to have seen him, and tried to make my words sound confused. "He was a rich man, I think, for he was dressed in fine kesut. Perhaps a caravan master."

"That sounds like the Hebrew merchant who was here earlier, bothering the master." Hlagor's eyes met mine, and there was a strange greed in them. "What of him?"

I thought desperately of my short conversation with Lappidoth. "This man spoke to me. He said something about fearing his rooms in town would be let to another because there are so many buyers in Hazor now."

"So? What care I if a Hebrew sleeps in the dirt?"

"He mentioned that there were no animals to be bought at the markets in Ephraim," I added quickly. "I thought that might be why so many have come."

"He could have lied, hoping to get a free bed." Hlagor stroked his chin. "Although I have not had time to go into town of late."

"Perhaps it would be wise to send a man to town," I suggested carefully. "They might seek out some of these merchants, and bring them to the farm to see our fine herd, and so buy what they wish from our master rather than another."

"Is that why you are babbling to me? Stupid girl, I have already made such a suggestion to the master," Hlagor said, but the gleam of excitement in his eyes could not be hidden. He had *not* thought of it, but now he would tell the master, and claim it as his own idea. "Now see to these animals, and clean up this mess." He hurried out of the barn.

I went to the window to watch him trot toward the main house. If Jeth had spoken the truth, Ybyon would immediately dispatch men to make rounds of the inns and taverns in the center of town. If Jeth had been exaggerating, Hlagor would be made to look foolish, and I would receive a sound thrashing.

Either way, Chemesh would not be killed. Not today, at least.

"Deborah."

I turned around and saw the other slaves. They stood still, waiting. I sought out Tarn's eyes, and saw in them what they all wanted, and I felt sick. "Must I?"

He nodded.

I was the smallest of the barn slaves, a woman, next to worthless because I could not do heavy work, and I was left-handed, which made me unlucky. Still, there was one thing I could do that the others could not. This was why they tolerated me, why they did not use me or harm me: my gift, which protected me even better than Meji, that made them fear me as much as they feared the master.

I hated using it this way, but after what had happened to Balaa, the men insisted on it. "Bring him to me, then."

Tarn and Meji took Chemesh by the arms and brought him before me.

"What? Why do you hold me?" He squirmed, and then gave me an ugly look. "You foolish wench. I would have beaten him bloody if you had not gotten in the way."

"Hlagor is the steward here, and a favorite of Ybyon, the master of us all," Tarn said. "Had you laid a finger on him, we would all have suffered."

Chemesh's face twisted into a sneer of contempt. "Why should you be punished for what I do?"

"It is the master's way." The lines around Tarn's mouth deepened. "Our food would have been stopped for days, our labors doubled, and our backs beaten. As for you, you would have been stripped, tied to the massebot, and flayed by the master's blade, alive, slowly, in front of all of us."

The anger faded from Chemesh's countenance. "How do you know this? It would not be so. What master would do such to his slaves?"

"A master who takes pleasure in our pain," Meji snapped. "The same one who starves us each day."

"We know because it has been done before to us," Tarn added. "Many times. Now you will be made known to us."

"Be made known? You already know me." Chemesh struggled, but the two men held him fast. "You are speaking foolishness, seba."

"We have nothing but each other." I gestured toward the slaves gathering around us. "Tarn is right; your moment of anger against Hlagor would have cost us all dearly. Now I must know who you are, and . . . see . . . what more you will do."

As Meji and Tarn held Chemesh still between them, I rested my left hand against the center of his forehead. My touch made him flinch with revulsion, but then he closed his eyes and did not move.

Tarn said my touch always held them as surely as iron chains.

I kept my eyes open and drew on my faith before I made my prayer to the One and True God, the Father of us all, the Lord who had given me this strange and fearful gift. *Jehovah, hear me now and help us live. Show me the path this one will walk. Show me the lives this one will touch. Show me all that he will be in this place.*

The world around me dimmed, and although my eyes remained open, they closed from within, and I went blind.

I was not afraid of this inner darkness. It was where I had to be for the dreams to come. It did not happen this way as it did in my sleep; waking dreams were much more powerful.

The essence of the one I touched grew like a flower, a tight bud that reached up from the darkness where all things living are born, and slowly began to open, filling me with its many tiny petals. The petals had voices made of images, and they sang to me in pictures of what had been, was, and what would be for Chemesh. Their songs were the soul of an angry, reckless man.

"Chemesh, blood of Rephah," I said, hearing the lonely wailing of the boy he had been, who had lost all his kin to plague. "Only child of Mino and Bekkala, both slaves. Your family comes from the west, where you served a fisherman of the Sea People. You know the water and the nets, but not the land." Light blended into the heaviness, but it was not a kind light. "You left behind a woman carrying your babe in her belly."

"Tlin," he whispered, his voice tight with anguish. "My wife."

"You were permitted to join, but then you were taken and sold on the public block for the price of repairing your master's boat. He would not sell your woman with you. A trader took you for his caravan east. Your anger comes from sorrow, from being torn from the one you loved." I saw why he had wanted more food. "You seek to steal provisions, weapons, and more clothing. You wish to escape this new master and make your way back to the sea. You will do whatever you must to make this so."

Chemesh gasped. "How can you know—?"

"Silence," Tarn thundered.

"You would have died this night," I said, seeing and hearing the fading petal song-image of what I had prevented. "You will court death again for the sake of Tlin's love, and for the babe she carries."

"Where does he go, Deborah?" Meji asked.

"Nowhere." The newest petals, those that told of Chemesh's life on the farm, had voices withered and ugly. "You will walk the circle of anger and sorrow, and have not a care for anyone, not even yourself, until you escape, or you can be with your woman and child again, or you are dead." I removed my hand from his face and spoke to Tarn and the others. "This bond between father, mother, and child cannot be broken. By the marriage, Jehovah has blessed it. We must help this man return to the land of his birth."

"Too risky," Tarn said. "He does not deserve it, and if we are caught, we will all be made to suffer."

"If we do not try," I warned, "Chemesh will not stop trying. In the end, he will die under the master's fist, and so will three more of us."

CHAPTER
5

Summoning a waking dream rendered me exhausted, and I left the matter for the men to worry over and staggered toward the heap of straw I used as my bed. *Tonight I sleep well,* I thought as I rolled over and hugged myself with my arms. Using my gift when I was awake sometimes allowed me to sleep like an untroubled child, but I had no control over the dreams after I fell asleep.

"Deborah."

Weight settled the straw beside me, and I looked up to see Meji's face. He seemed almost angry. "Tell Tarn that I cannot see more of Chemesh until I have rested," I said.

"Tarn does not need you. We have decided to smuggle the new one out tomorrow night, when the feed wagon delivers the grain the master ordered." He brushed a strand of hair back from my face. "You liked that man who came here today, didn't you?"

I had liked Jeth, more than I should have, but I only moved my shoulders. It was not for me to like or dislike such a man.

Meji turned his face away and stared through the open window at the night sky. "You were born to the wrong mother. You belong with someone like him."

"Only if he buys me from the master." Which would never happen, and I smothered a yawn. "Are you cold? Do you wish to sleep with me tonight?" I moved over to make a place for him in the straw.

"You are too restless." He took my hand in his. "If he comes again, you should find a way to speak with him."

"And risk a beating? Why?"

His fingers tightened over mine. "If you interest him enough, he might buy you from the master."

I snorted. "Yes, I can see how he might want a slave clever enough to be caught outside in a hailstorm. I cannot imagine why he did not run to the house as soon as the ice stopped falling and beg the master to sell me to him." Why did Meji keep bringing up Jeth? "He is a rich man, and likely has many fine slaves. He does not need me."

He made a sad sound. "You see so much, but never yourself."

I almost reached out to touch him with my left hand, so that I could know what he meant, but as a rule, I tried not to see just for my own curiosity. Also, my gift had limits. If I did another seeing, I would have trouble waking in the morning, and I could not afford to miss the morning meal again.

"I am too tired to see anything but the insides of my eyelids," I told him. "Come, lie down with me, and sleep. I will try not to toss and turn too much."

"Very well." Meji stretched out behind me, curling his limbs into mine and resting his hand on my hip. "Have only good dreams this night, my friend."

I closed my burning eyes and sighed. If I were fortunate, I would have no dreams at all.

As soon as I drifted off, my luck turned, and I became the flower that grew, the petals that sang in their wordless way. I struggled against the sleeping dream, for there was something in it, something large and dark and terrifying, and it wanted me.

Why do you abide among the sheepfolds, a great and furious voice said, *to hear only the bleating of the flocks?*

I was alone with it, this terrible thing, and I could not run away from its wrath. *I am but a slave. I cannot abide but where my master wills it.* I stopped trying to flee and opened my heart, and knew the One and True God's presence within me. *Tell me Your will, Heavenly Father. I am your servant in all things.*

What was terrible became at once gentle and forgiving. *Your burden is heavy, daughter, but it is not all that you know.*

I could hear the bleating of lambs at play, and felt the softness of wool on my fingers. The warmth of the sun touched my face, and the taste of sweet dates spread over my tongue. I could see Meji's smile, deep, green grass, and the little red flowers that sometimes sprang up around the barn. All the things that were beautiful in life filled my heart with love, a love that surrounded me and comforted me against that which was harsh and hurtful.

Yes, I understand now. I am grateful for my life, Father of Heaven.

Then you must listen to your heart, seer of dreams. Listen and follow, and you shall know what you must do, and where you belong.

I saw Jeth's kind face, and felt the unseen connection between us for the first time. That grew into a vision of a palm tree, of a kind I had never seen. We sat together on a striped cloth spread beneath it, our hands entwined, our faces turned toward each other. We were speaking, but I could not hear what Jeth or I said. Then a shadow fell over us, and lightning flashed between us, and our hands parted.

This strange vision of peace and terror frightened me, and yet it turned something deep inside me. Was this part of my purpose? I could not have been made this way for no reason. I beseeched Jehovah to guide me again. *What does this mean, Father? What must I do?*

Save the shepherd, and lead the lightning, daughter, the deep voice said, and My garden will be yours.

All these things faded into darkness, and I woke from the disturbing dream, cold despite the warmth of Meji's body next to mine. Although the sky had yet to lighten with the coming dawn, I rose and went to the stalls to look after the animals. My dream made little sense, but something had changed inside me. Perhaps it was knowing that the Father was watching over me, or the strange prophecy He had given me.

Save the shepherd. Lead the lightning.

I had just finished milking the last of the goats when I heard voices outside, and went to the window to see if our morning meal had been brought.

"We should wait for him to journey to the river," Hlagor was saying in a low, urgent voice. "We can tie stones to the body and dispose of it there."

"The king cares not for what happens to a foreigner wandering the streets of Hazor," Ybyon replied. "You will go into town tonight."

The steward made an impatient sound. "You are not taking the risk. If the king's guard catches me with stolen silver, it will be my head on a pike."

Quick laughter rang out. "You fool. How can the silver be stolen if the Hebrew who owned it is dead?"

I covered my mouth with my hand to smother a gasp of horror and revulsion. They were speaking of Jeth—of killing him for his silver.

"I do not like this," Hlagor muttered. "He is young and strong-looking, not like the others you have had me kill. He will fight for his life."

"That is why you will drink with him first." Cloth rustled. "Have the tavern keeper put these herbs in his wine cup. The midwife gave them to my wife during her last labor, and she was befuddled for two days after."

I sagged back against the wall. This was why Ybyon had not killed him before; he had wanted Jeth's silver more than his life. I had always known my master possessed an evil heart, but this scheme was so dishonorable, it took my breath away. The Hebrew merchant, who had come to Hazor only to buy sheep, who had shown me only kindness, would die tonight, and there was nothing I could do to stop it. I saw Chemesh surreptitiously scoop a handful of grain from a feed trough and put it in his mouth.

Or is there?

"You have brain fever," Meji said flatly.

"Perhaps." I crouched beside him and took one of the ewe's two teats to squeeze it gently. Milk squirted into the shallow pan I held in my other hand. "It makes no difference. I must still go and do this thing."

All through the day I had been unable to stop thinking about Jeth, or my master's plan to have Hlagor murder him in town. I was not permitted to leave the farm, nor was there anyone with whom I could send word to the Hebrew merchant to warn him that his life was in danger. It was seeing Chemesh eating fodder that made me think of running away.

My plan seemed even more sensible when Tarn mentioned the next morning that Chemesh had developed bad bowels, probably from eating too much raw grain, and was now too sick to work. I agreed to do a share of Chemesh's work so that he would not be beaten for it, and then asked Tarn if I could use the escape plan to go into town.

"You will never make it back before dawn," the old slave warned me. "Hlagor will have the wagon. You will be on foot." He touched his neck. "The master will not stop at scarring you. He will take great delight in parting you from your skin. Slowly, and completely."

I had little doubt of that, but then I thought of Balaa, and how I had felt for weeks after his slow death. I had not foreseen his fate, but it did not make me feel any better. I could not allow my master's greed and hatred to

destroy another life—even if it meant sacri-
ficing my own. "I know what I do, Tarn."

I had tried to convince Meji of the same
thing, but he would have none of it. "You cannot go into town. As soon as the morning
meal is brought, you will be missed. Hlagor
knows you spoke to the man. You will be
blamed for betraying the master."

"You cannot betray a murderer." I finished
milking the ewe and handed the warm pan
of milk to him. "Will you help me do this?"

"I should strangle you now, and save the
master the trouble." He put the pan aside
and ground the heels of his hands into his
eyes for a moment before scowling at me.
"Deborah, you do not even know this man.
You owe him nothing. To sacrifice your life for
his . . . it is beyond foolishness."

"I told you what I dreamed. I do not understand it all, but this is the will of Jehovah." I
wiped my wet hands with some straw, and I
rose. "Never mind. I have already spoken to
Tarn. He will help me do what needs be
done."

"No." His voice went from harsh to quiet.
"No, if you are to play this part, you will
need me."

I was not a vain female, but I felt like

squirming a little more than an hour later, when Meji smeared a thick mixture of wood charcoal and torch grease into my hair to darken it.

"Keep it hanging over your eyes," he said as he tucked my now-greasy braid under the back of my middo. Before I could thank him, he moved away, his shoulders rigid with anger.

"It is because he cares for you," Tarn said, watching him leave the barn. "You must be careful to whom in town you speak, Deborah. The king's soldiers patrol the streets, and they are always arresting and interrogating anyone who acts suspiciously. Keep your voice low, for you do not sound much like a boy." He described how the soldiers dressed, and added, "Some are brutes from the west, and enjoy using female prisoners for their pleasure. If they call to you, run away."

I felt sick in my belly now. "When will the feed wagon arrive?"

His cloudy eyes went to the door Meji had left hanging open, and checked the position of the sun. "Within the hour. You have not much time to finish."

I had no polished circle of brass to look

into, as the master's wife did, so I filled a bucket with water to look upon my reflection. The blackish muck and the way Meji had trimmed the front of my hair did make me resemble a Canaanite boy—one who had been rolling in the mud. I also smeared my face and arms with fresh dirt, hoping it would complete my street urchin disguise.

"Here." Meji came and thrust some clothing into my hands. "The master's son threw these away some weeks ago. I was saving them for . . . but it matters not now. Wear them."

"I thank you." The garments were shabby and old, but finer than anything I had ever worn. I stepped behind a stall gate to change. "I will find a way home, Meji, even if I must hide myself on Hlagor's wagon."

"Do not bother to come back."

My chin dropped. "What?"

"You heard me." He made a quick gesture in the direction of town. "Go to this Hebrew, and tell him of the plot against him as you planned, but stay with him. He will be grateful enough to take you with him. You will be safe in Ephraim."

"I cannot impose myself on a stranger. I know nothing of him." As I pulled on the short kuttonet and kesut, I refused to think of the image from my dream, of sitting with Jeth beneath the strange palm. "Even if I did, if I were to escape the master, he would take out his anger on the rest of you. I cannot permit that."

"He will rage at us whether you come back or not. Better I take a beating for your liberty than for your death." Meji's mouth became a bitter twist, and he lifted his hand to my braid to tuck it out of sight under the collar of the kesut. "I put too much dye at your brow, it is going to run. Close your eyes for a moment."

I did so, and flinched as I felt warm breath, then a mouth against my mouth. Before I could gasp, the kiss was over.

"Meji." I touched my lips, my eyes wide.

"I have cared for you since we were children." He caressed my cheek. "If we were free, you are the only one I would take as wife, but no son of mine will be born under the yoke, or sold away from me on the block." His hand fell away. "There is no reason to be sad. When I was small, just before your mother died, she told me how it would be with us. She knew as well as I that you would leave here with another."

My mother had spoken to him of this?

"I did not know. I will never leave here. No one wants me." The thought of running away seemed as ludicrous as wedding Meji. He was the closest thing I had to a brother. "I am sorry."

"So am I." He looked over at the rattling, creaking sounds of the feed wagon as it approached the barn. "Come. It is time."

CHAPTER
6

Our plan was a simple one. Chemesh was too ill to risk trying to smuggle off the farm in the feed wagon, so I would take his place. Once the wagon reached town, I would go to the inn of Dhiban and find Jeth.

I slipped out of the side door of the barn and hid myself in the shadows, trembling with nerves as I waited and listened for the signal from Tarn. Hlagor was already gone, but the master might come down from the house to inspect the delivery. Night had not yet fallen. If he saw me with my hair darkened and dressed thus, or even noticed that I was gone . . .

"Shall I bring water for your oxen, Adon?" I heard Tarn ask.

I crept around the side of the barn. The driver's attention was on Tarn, and there was no one else near the wagon. This was my best chance. As silently as I could manage, I hurried over to the wagon and climbed into the back, crawling under the pile of emptied feed sacks until I had wedged myself against the board behind the driver's planked seat. I pulled some of the sacks back and over me until I was completely covered with them.

"No, seba, I watered them at the last stop." The board creaked under my shoulder blades as the driver climbed onto the seat.

I dared not move again until the wagon was under way. The feed sacks were dusty with fragments of seed and chaff, and I breathed through my mouth so that I would not be tempted to sneeze. Relief surged through me when I heard the driver slap his reins against the oxen's broad backs. He had not noticed me. I would be able to escape the farm and find Jeth in Hazor.

What if Hlagor has already killed him?

"Hold."

The wagon, which had just begun to roll away from the barn, came to a stop.

"You delivered ten measures of feed grain?" I heard Ybyon ask, not a foot away from where I lay hiding.

"I did. The old one with the scarred neck watched me fill your bins," the driver said. "Ten measures were all that were ordered."

"I see." Ybyon sounded as if he did not. "My slaves did not ask you to deliver anything to town? A passenger?"

I curled my fingernails into my palms. *Please, Lord God, do not let him find me.*

"I haul grain," the driver told him. "Not people."

The sound of the master's heavy footsteps moved to the end of the wagon, and I heard some sacks being shifted. Did he see the outline of my form under the sacks? I did not dare breathe, for if Ybyon found me cringing beneath them—

"Give my regards to your master," my master said, and the driver grunted before the wagon began to roll again.

I did not mind the smothering wad of sacks covering my head. I thought nothing of the jolting of the wagon as it traveled down the farm road. I had escaped Ybyon, and if Jehovah were generous, I would find Jeth before Hlagor did.

After a few minutes, I dared shift one of the sacks to peek out. Behind the wagon, the grass and weed-patched pastures of my master had become the pale dirt of a well-traveled road. The wagon did not rattle so much now, but splinters of wood from the board behind me pierced my skin, and I had to keep myself braced by hands and feet to keep from tumbling over. The temptation to jump off the wagon was strong, but on such a deserted road, the driver might see me and force me to return to the farm.

I had to wait, or all would be lost.

Fear became my master on that ride into town, which seemed to be endless. Hlagor might already have Jeth sitting with him in a tavern and drinking wine drugged with the master's herbs. I had not thought of what I would do if I found the two men together. My voice would betray me; Hlagor knew my face just as well. Perhaps I could send another to summon the Hebrew merchant away from the steward. But who would play messenger for a runaway slave playing the part of a dirty street urchin?

I dared not attempt a waking dream; it would leave me weak, perhaps helpless. Instead, I held myself still and prayed for patience.

Voices, the creaking of other wheels, and the sounds of mules, sheep, and other animals told me that the wagon had at last reached the center of town, but I made a gap in the sacks over me to have a look. Light from large torches atop thick poles that had been driven into the ground on either side of the road flared against a clear, dark sky. Faint, twinkling stars were just beginning to appear in the purple twilight. Like the standing torches, walls built of mud brick loomed over every side of the wagon, and some were so crooked, I thought they would collapse on me at any moment. My panic faded as another wagon passed close by, and I realized the street upon which we traveled must be very narrow.

Town did not smell like the farm. The odors of straw, animals, and manure were fainter, muted by the smells of people, privies, fire, and cooking food. There were also other, foreign scents I did not know, that were sharp, spicy, and sour in turns. The air seemed thicker and warmer here, as well, but the walls likely blocked some of the cold winter winds.

My mouth sagged as I saw a shabbily robed man pause in a space between two walls, lift the front of his simla, and make his water on the ground. He did so without hesitation, right there where anyone could see him. Others walked past him, evidently unconcerned.

No wonder Hazor smells like an open privy, I thought as the wagon turned a corner. *The people use it as one.*

I did not know how much farther the driver had to travel, but I did not wish to wait until his final stop to get off. I kept the sacks over me and crawled slowly on my hands and belly toward the edge of the wagon bed. When the driver passed through a shadowed area between two of the standing torches, I shook off the sacks and slid from the wagon to the ground.

Ugh. I knew from the feel and the smell that both of my feet had landed in a chilly mixture of mud and manure. I did not wait to scrape it off, but hurried to the nearest dark niche I could find. The door within the mud-brick entry was closed, but I stood there only until the wagon had disappeared from my sight before stepping out onto the street.

Jehovah save us. I tried not to stare as I

walked along, but my eyes wanted to jump out of my head. I had never seen so many people in such a small place. Even during the coldest nights, when we brought the flock from the sheepfold into the barns and lean-tos to shelter them against the freezing air, it was not this crowded.

The people of Hazor paid as much attention to me as they had the man making his water in the street. Some walked in groups, clustered together, as grapes on the vine, while others traveled in pairs or alone. Most were men in robes, but I saw a number wearing slave middo, and common laborers with their chests and arms bare, their stomachs and hips covered by a short cloth ezor knotted on one side. Some had ezor belted with a wide leather hagora, upon which hung a short sheath and sword, and I knew those to be the soldiers Tarn had worried might capture me. To run from them would only draw their attention, so I kept my head down and walked at an even, steady pace.

I saw some women wearing long head veils and flowing kesut of many colors that covered them from shoulder to foot. They also had at least one man escorting them, as befitted a respectable female. There were few children in the streets—I knew from my master's family that Canaanites were protective of their young ones, and did not permit them to wander off unattended—but those I saw did not wear the middo of the slave-born.

Tarn had told me that beggars were restricted from entering Hazor and lived outside the walls of town, but I saw a number of free men who looked hungry and dirty, and who loitered nervously outside several doorways. One that I passed opened, and the man inside tossed out scraps of bread in a careless fashion. Before the door closed again, the waiting poor went down on their hands and knees on the muddy ground, scrambling to snatch up what crusts their hands had missed.

I averted my gaze, for I knew the shame of being so hungry that even mud-soiled bread was a blessing.

"Baal's Eye, what a stink." Something pushed at the back of my left shoulder, and a soft, flowery scent teased my nose. "Did you fall into a herd of sheep, boy, or what they left behind?"

I glanced back and saw a broad, smiling face surrounded by short, gleaming brown curls. The man was short, with a thick body and prominent belly, but dressed in finely embroidered robes. His features had been colored with some of the same exotic Egyptian cosmetics that Ybyon's wife wore, and the flower smell was coming from his person. I would have thought him a woman, if not for the style of his kesut and the high, pointed head covering with its hanging tassels, something that only the men of town wore.

"N–neither, zaqen." I could not call free men *Adon* here, or I would betray myself as a slave. I kept walking, hoping the odd fellow would not follow me.

"Your stench is formidable." The man caught up to me and touched my arm. "Fortunately, I have a tub and plenty of water jugs, soap, and perfumed oil. I also like to play maid. How much for this night?"

He wished to buy the night? I shook my head, afraid to speak again.

The man pulled me to a stop and peered at my face and neck. "By Dagon, my eyes are easily deceived. What do you here, young one? Have you taken leave of your senses, to be wandering alone in this quarter?"

"I do not live here—my father is a merchant from the south, and we arrived this morning," I lied in the lowest voice I could manage. "We became separated today at market. He has rooms at the inn of Dhiban, but I am lost and cannot find it."

"Indeed." The red-stained lips pursed. "You have but to walk down two streets"—he pointed in one direction as he spoke—"then turn the corner right, and you will be standing before Dhiban's inn."

My gratitude and relief were so sharp that my knees almost buckled. "I thank you, zaqen."

"I will walk with you and keep you company." The man patted my arm. "Your father should be praised for rearing such a polite, determined, ah, person as you are. I am Parah, scribe and poet to whoever can afford my talents."

I could not run away from him; he knew my destination. There were two king's guards standing on the other side of the street, and one of them was looking in my direction.

I made my mouth smile. "It is not necessary to trouble yourself, Zaqen Parah."

"Nonsense." He waved one hand back and forth. "What is your name?"

"Meji." It was the only male name that came into my head. "Your guidance was all the help I needed. And I think my father may be, ah, asleep by now. He was very tired."

"Sleeping? While his beloved Meji is missing?" Parah shook his head so that his curls bounced. "Surely not."

I could not think of what more to say, so I began to walk again.

The stout scribe strolled beside me and kept talking, although much of what he said made little sense to me. "There are so many merchants and caravanners in town this month that none of my regulars are available. Then there are the Sea People, always sending their envoys and dignitaries here to bedevil our poor king, who must of course entertain them to keep the salt and purple dye flowing west. They say the torches at the palace blaze from dusk until midday. I would take my household and business and move south, if it were not for the Hebrews. My kind, they would doubtless hang from the first tree."

"Your kind, Zaqen Parah?" I had to ask.

"Let me not enlighten you on that, Meji. There are some things that should remain a mystery to innocence." He patted my arm again. "It will take days for you to wash that atrocious dye out of your hair, you know. Who wished you to look like an Egyptian beggar? Not this father, I hope. I shall have to thrash him."

"No, it was . . ." I remembered I had taken Meji's name. "A friend." I almost touched my head before I remembered the cinder-and-fat mixture. "I like it dark."

He chuckled. "You will never catch a husband looking like a Nubian boy." I stumbled, and he put a surprisingly strong arm around me. "There, there, child, don't look as if you mean to flee down the hill. Your breasts are small enough to be missed under that loose robe, but your braid slipped out of your collar one block back. There is not a man or boy in this town with hair that long." He took my betraying braid and tucked it back under my kesut. "So, Meji, if that is your name, why do you pretend to be what you are not?"

I wanted to tear out my wayward hair. "I cannot say. You will summon the king's guards."

Parah laughed now. "I have no liking for those brutes, and I will not leave you alone until you tell me what you are about. I am not an innocent, you see, and as such, I am completely unable to resist such a mystery."

I was putting myself and Jeth in danger by doing so, but I suspected only the truth would satisfy this odd scribe.

"My name is not Meji, as you have guessed, and I am not a boy, and the man I go to see is not my father," I admitted. "He is a stranger visiting Hazor from Ephraim to buy sheep for his herds. There are men I know who wish to do him harm and steal his silver. I must warn him if I can."

Parah's amusement faded. "Gods, child, what a tale. And I can see the truth in your eyes now." He looked one way down the street and then the other. "It will do no good to bring the king's men into this; such matters are better handled with discretion. We will go to Dhiban's inn and find the man directly. What is his name?"

"Lappidoth. He also calls himself Jeth."

"The Hebrew." He did not wait for me to confirm this. "He hired me to record his purchases. A good sort, I thought, even if his people are bent on conquering Canaan one town at a time." He eyed me. "Your name?"

"Deborah."

"Another Hebrew name." He picked up one of my hands and turned it over to run a thumb over the calluses on my palm. "You have the hands of a hard worker—or a slave."

"I am not running away," I said quickly. "I only wish to keep our steward from killing this man. When I have warned Jeth, and he is safe, I will return to my master's farm."

Parah gave me a shrewd look. "Yes, I can see that you would. Come, then, Deborah. We must make haste."

CHAPTER
7

Parah said no more, and his step quickened as we hurried toward Dhiban's inn. One young man called out to him from the window of a brightly painted building where men were going in and out, but the scribe only waved a hand and held on to my arm. It was seeing the painted face of the boy, and some of the others looking down from the windows on the second floor, that distracted me.

"What is that place, Zaqen Parah?" I gestured back to it.

"A brothel." He tugged me around a half-frozen puddle and pulled his robe closer around his neck with the other hand, shuddering as a cold wind found its way through the labyrinth of walls and alleyways.

I did not know the word. "What is that?"

He gave me a sideways glance and uttered a laugh. "You *are* a farm girl, are you not? A brothel is a house of pleasure, where men go when they wish to buy time with a woman. You do know what men and women do together when they are wed?" He waited for my nod. "Those who work in a brothel are paid to do the same."

"But those people were all men." I glanced back to be sure. "Do women go there to pay for them?"

Parah laughed so hard, I thought he might do himself an injury. "Ah, Deborah," he gasped when he could control his mirth, "I might have to buy you from your master and keep you for my own amusement. No, child, women never go there. Some men who do not care for the comforts of women do."

It took me a moment to work it out. "Oh, like the goat shepherds."

He smiled and took my arm to steer me around a corner. "Hmmm. I have heard such men called goats more than once, but never goat *shepherds*."

"I speak of two men at my master's farm

who care for each other that way. They were bought from a tribe of desert nomads. I once saw two of them exchange a kiss when they thought themselves alone." I shrugged. "I spoke of it to Tarn, the oldest of our farm-workers. He told me that among our people such things are forbidden, but he himself did not condemn them. Love and comfort are blessed things." I thought of Ybyon. "There is so little of it in the world."

"I cannot argue that fact. Here, now, that is Dhiban's inn." He pointed to a narrow building with a smoke-darkened fleece hanging from a rod atop the entry way. "Your Hebrew friend will be inside?"

"I do not know. He may." I gnawed at my lower lip and looked for Ybyon's wagon, but did not see it or Hlagor. "If my master's steward sees me, and seizes me, will you find Jeth, and tell him what I have said?"

"No one will seize you if we better your costume." Parah removed his headdress, gave it a distinctly resigned look, and then placed it over my muddy head. "There. It covers some of the smell, too, for which my nose has much gratitude. Walk behind me and hold your tongue. I will question the innkeeper."

He had not exposed me, he had escorted me here, and now he had ruined his fine head covering. "Why are you being so kind to me?"

Parah tugged up his sleeve and displayed what appeared to be a scar from a terrible burn on his forearm. "Do you know how to remove a slave brand?"

"Only by cutting away the flesh—" I stopped, and my eyes moved from his arm to his face. "You mean you were—?"

"It takes many weeks to heal, but if you keep the wound clean and dry, it will." He dropped his sleeve and strode into the entry.

Feeling unnerved and somewhat dazed by his revelation, I followed.

The dim, smoky air within Dhiban's made it hard to see at first, and then my eyes grew accustomed to the murky interior. Parah and I had entered a common room where several men were eating and drinking at a long table fashioned of loose planks laid across flat-topped, crudely carved stone pillars. Torches on all sides of the room generated the greasy smoke, some of which escaped through three small open windows. The smoke could not quite cover the smell of sweat, burnt meat, and sour beer.

"Innkeeper," Parah called out, clapping his hands together sharply.

I stayed behind the scribe, keeping my eyes downcast and trying not to attract any attention.

A large man wearing a stained ezor tied around his hips with a length of frayed cord limped up to stand before Parah, whom he gave an insolent look.

"You come to the wrong place." The innkeeper perched the heavy wine jug in his hands on one broad hip. "I do not let rooms for the hour."

"I come here looking for a merchant who buys sheep," the scribe said. "A tall, spotless fellow from the south country. He has dark hair and good robes. I must arrange delivery of the purchase tablets he hired me to write for him."

Dhiban scanned the room. "He is not here. Try again tomorrow."

"Did you see this man leave the inn with anyone?" Parah persisted. "It may be that he went to a tavern with a mutual friend."

"Perhaps he did. I have no time to watch who comes and goes." Dhiban's gaze moved to me, and his expression turned to disgust. "You brought that boy for him?"

"No, this is my apprentice," Parah lied. "I brought him to see how the final sale is done. He has much to learn."

"With you as his master?" Dhiban shook his head. "Gods help you, boy." He went to the table and began refilling the men's cups with wine.

Parah looked at the stairway that led up to the second floor, where the inn's rooms were located. "We should go and see if he is in his rooms, and if not, then we will start searching the local taverns." He grimaced. "There are only three or four dozen."

"You are looking for Jeth?" a coy female voice asked.

We both turned to see a woman who looked like a younger, female version of Dhiban. She wore no veil, and her middo and striped kesut proclaimed her an unmarried daughter, but her girth was nearly equal to that of the innkeeper's.

"Yes, keli," Parah said. "Do you know where he has gone?"

"Nowhere yet this night." She giggled at the scribe's address—doubtless the first time anyone had ever called her a jewel—and waved toward what had to be the kitchen. "He wished to eat alone, so I served him his dinner at the family's table."

I wanted to run in, but Parah gave me a warning glance. "Thank you, keli. I will praise your kindness to the Gods this night."

The innkeeper's daughter blushed and giggled this time before going to help her father serve the men in the front room.

"Slowly, child," the scribe murmured to me. "If you dash in there, it may look suspicious to someone watching."

Was Hlagor among the innkeeper's guests? I glanced back at the men at the table, but did not see the steward's face.

Parah heaved a sigh. "Fearful looks are also rather betraying." He cupped my elbow and led me into the kitchen.

Dhiban's kitchen was not as large or as clean as my master's, and there was only a single cooking pit that was shallow and blackened from many old fires. Jeth was there, as the innkeeper's daughter had said, sitting at a smaller version of the common room's table and finishing a meal of soup, lehem, and dried fruit. When he saw us, he stood up politely and bowed.

"I am nearly done here," he said, and then

recognition made his expression change. "Scribe Parah, I did not expect to see you here until the morning. Was there some difficulty with recording the purchase?"

"Yes." The scribe went to the kitchen door and closed it. "The purchase will not take place tomorrow. The man from whom you bought sheep does not plan to deliver the animals. He intends to have you robbed and murdered tonight."

Jeth appeared shocked into silence. Finally he made a conciliatory gesture. "I think you must be confused about this, to make such a scandalous accusation. Ybyon came very highly recommended to me."

"Whoever sent you to him must have wished you harm," Parah told him, "for that is all that will come of your dealings with this man."

"He speaks the truth, Adon," I said, taking off Parah's head covering. "If you wish to live, you must flee Hazor tonight."

"You are the girl from the barn—Deborah." His eyes widened as he took in my appearance. "Jehovah preserve us, what have you done to yourself?"

"She has run away from her master and put her life in great danger to give you this warning," Parah snapped. "I suggest you heed it."

Jeth came over to me. "Why would you say such a thing about Ybyon? Who told you this story?"

"No one. I heard it myself," I assured him. "I was there when my master gave his steward orders to rob and kill you."

"What do you here, girl?" His expression changed, and he turned to Parah. "Slaves sometimes lie to create mischief and avenge themselves on their masters."

"But Hebrews do not," I reminded him. "Falsehood is a grievous sin in the eyes of God, as Moses taught our people, and as the Hebrew slaves who raised me taught me."

"How happy am I that He is not my god, then," Parah said.

"He is the One and True God. There is no other." The distraction made me exasperated. "Adon Lappidoth, you must hear me. My master, Ybyon, has sent his steward, Hlagor, to find you. Hlagor will be friendly and ask you to drink with him—only when you cannot see, he will put herbs in your cup that will make you addle-headed and unable to defend yourself. Then Hlagor intends to steal your silver, take you down to the river, and slay you there."

"But why kill me? I have not cheated Ybyon," Jeth protested. "Nor have I committed any offense against him or his kin. What have I done to deserve such brutal treatment?"

Before I could tell him of how my master's family had been lost during the fall of Jericho, the very thing I most feared happened: Hlagor came in.

"Adon Lappidoth, here you are," he said, smiling broadly. "My master, Ybyon, bade me come to speak with you."

I turned my back toward the steward before he could see my face, and I gave Parah a beseeching look.

"I am speaking business with Lappidoth now, slave," the scribe said, folding his arms. "You can wait outside until we are through."

"What business is this?" Hlagor demanded.

"A matter of some urgency," Jeth said. "If you would go out and have the innkeeper pour some wine for us, I will join you shortly."

I could feel the steward's suspicious gaze moving over my back, and held my breath.

"As you say, Adon," Hlagor muttered. "I will wait."

As soon as the door closed, I whirled around. "Why did you tell him to get wine for you? Did you not hear what I said? Do you *wish* to die?"

"It was only to make him leave. I will not drink any wine tonight, Deborah. I rarely do even when men are not plotting my death." Jeth stroked his short beard with one hand as he thought. "I can deal with this steward, but what of your master? He already has half my payment for the sheep he promised to deliver to me tomorrow night. I cannot return to Ephraim empty-handed; some of the silver I carry belongs to neighbors who could not make the journey. These animals are desperately needed by our tribe."

"As long as you are still breathing come tomorrow, and have in your possession the remainder of the payment," Parah said, "Ybyon must bring the sheep to you or risk losing the animals and the payment under forfeiture law. Until it is time for the delivery, you will come and stay at my home. My staff is well-trained and will guard you closely, and in the morn, I will be your witness and assure the deal is closed fairly."

I saw Jeth was still caught up in disbelief, and I put my hand on his sleeve. "Adon, please. It is the truth. I swear it."

"I had better go and entertain that steward, else he come back here looking for you," Parah said. "You know where my home is, Hebrew. I will meet you there." To me, the scribe said, "Remember what I showed you, child, and take care—your life is in as much danger as his."

I held out his head covering, but Parah only laughed, shook his head, and left the kitchen.

"First ice from the sky, and now murder from the shadows," Jeth murmured. "Calamity seems to follow you, Deborah."

"More oft I am trying to run from it." I sighed. "I am sorry to bring tidings of such terrible things, but I could not stand by and do nothing."

"I can see that." A rueful smile curled Jeth's mouth. "How many women would dye their hair and run away from a master to warn a stranger? You know nothing of me. I might have turned you over to the king's guard."

"No," I said quietly, thinking of the many dreams I had had of this man. "I know you."

He looked puzzled. "How so? We have never met."

I could not tell him about the dreams; he

would think me mad. "If you meant me ill, you would not have treated me with such kindness during the hailstorm." I felt my cheeks grow hot and felt as ridiculous as the innkeeper's giggling daughter. "There is more that I should tell you about Ybyon. His family was almost wiped out during the fall of Jericho. The few relations who survived taught him from boyhood to hate Hebrews. That is why he buys so many of us as slaves, and why he wants you dead."

His eyes narrowed with anger. "And why you are so thin, and so fearful. He has been abusing you and the others, has he not?"

"A slave's life is never one of luxury and idleness." I did not want to make Jeth angry, not with Hlagor waiting in the next room. "You should go now."

He did not move an inch. "I must settle the debt between us first."

"There is no debt—"

"Surely my life is not worthless," he chided. "Given Ybyon's hatred of our people, I doubt he would sell you to me, but perhaps I could give Parah the funds to buy you and set you free." He frowned. "Why do you shake your head so? Do you not wish for freedom?"

"You would repay me by making *my* life worthless." Bitterness filled me with a cold and terrible despair. "I have no family, and no place else to live. Your gift of freedom would make me into a beggar, and I would be driven from Hazor. I would end up starving like the other gerum at the town gates." Convinced that Hlagor would barge in at any moment, I gestured toward the door. "I tell you that there is no debt. Forget about me and leave this place."

"I can do one, but not the other." He put his hand on my shoulder. "Come with me. I will conceal you, and I will take you from this place. I will care for you." His thumb glided down the side of my neck. "I think you will come to care for me."

How I wanted to say yes. My skin prickled where he touched me, and a peculiar ache lodged under my breastbone. Never had I felt more open to another—as if he had unlocked something inside me, something I had never recognized as part of myself. My mouth went dry, and my legs trembled.

Meji's narrow, bitter face came into my thoughts, and once again I heard him speak of my dead mother's prophecy to him. *She knew as well as I that you would leave here with another.*

If I escaped Ybyon and Hazor with Jeth, Meji and the other slaves would be punished, perhaps killed in my place. Preventing that was more important than indulging in a forbidden desire for this stranger.

"I cannot go with you, Adon Lappidoth," I said with great difficulty. "I thank you for offering."

"I will not leave you a beggar," he assured me. "You would stay with me. I will take you to Ephraim, and provide for you."

Before he could make more ridiculous promises, I said, "My master provides for me. Not very much, but enough to live on. If I left with you, others would suffer in my place, and that I cannot permit." I moved past him, but I did not wish us to part on my ungrateful refusal. I paused and added, "Jehovah watch over you, Adon."

Then I ran from the inn and into the alley, where I found Hlagor's empty wagon waiting.

I could not believe my luck—here was my way to return to the farm; all I needed was to climb into the back and keep low; in the darkness the steward would never see me. I could jump off as soon as we left the road and run across the fields to the barn.

I felt anxious but relieved, and absently tucked Parah's head covering over my sticky, dirty hair. I would have such tales to tell the others when I returned. Meji would enjoy hearing about the scribe—he had always wished to learn to read and write—

The weight of a hand settled on my right shoulder, and I heaved an exasperated sigh as I turned. "Adon Lappidoth, what must I do to—?" I looked into calm, familiar eyes, and the remaining words died in my throat.

"I think you have done enough," Ybyon said softly, picking up my braid from where it had escaped my kesut again. "Deborah."

CHAPTER
8

I was going to die, of that I had no doubt. My master had shoved a rag into my mouth to keep me from calling out, and had tied my wrists and ankles together with a thick rope to keep me from running away. I could only lie in the back of the wagon where he had tossed me and listen for the sound of voices, and hope none of them were Jeth's.

"I do not know how she escaped the farm," Hlagor's voice suddenly came from behind me. "I checked the wagon before I left the stable. There was nothing in the back."

"She must have hidden herself under the sacks on the grain wagon," my master said, his voice moving around me. "I thought it looked too low to the ground. The driver was careless and did not watch while the men were unloading."

I closed my eyes. The driver was not a slave, but he might be held responsible for my actions. *Jehovah, grant him Your protection.*

"What of the Hebrew merchant?" my master was asking Hlagor.

"He vanished from the kitchen while that scribe was distracting me. I know not where—" There was the sound of a fist hitting flesh, and a heavy weight crashed into the side of the wagon. Hlagor grunted and spat. "Do not put this on my head. I did as you told me. The little witch got to him before I could."

"If you had done as I told you, that cursed Hebrew would be dead, and my pockets filled with his silver." There was the sound of another blow. "I should kill you here and leave you in the gutter for the rats."

"Then who will do your killing for you?" Hlagor gasped out the words. "You have lost your taste for it."

I squeezed my eyes shut as I heard the ugly sounds of a vicious beating.

"Wait." The steward wheezed, and the

wagon rocked. "It is not my doing. She must possess the same witchery as her mother, else she would not know to come to warn him."

"Has she?" There were no more thuds of flesh against flesh, but Ybyon's voice changed and became thoughtful. "Her mother told me not."

The steward made a contemptuous sound. "Dasah deceived you to protect her brat. She always did pamper the girl."

"She told me the girl did nothing but dream." My master fell silent. "Get her up from there, that I may speak to her."

Hands grabbed my kesut and dragged me up on my knees. Hlagor's mouth was dripping blood, and there was murder on his battered face as he clamped one of his big hands around my neck.

"Tell him," the steward ordered, and shook me hard. "Tell our master what spell you cast to see into our thoughts."

"Wait." Ybyon took the rag from my mouth. "Now her tongue might work."

I swallowed against a tight, dry throat. "Adon, I do not understand. I am not a witch. I do not know how to cast spells." It was not a lie. My gift had nothing to do with evil or magic.

Incredibly, he nodded. "But you see things, though, do you not? Things that you know will happen, as your mother did. Can you do so as she could, whenever you wish?"

I would not say yes, so I said nothing.

"You need not fear me, girl," my master said, in the gentle way he had of speaking when he was most enraged. "Tell me where the Hebrew will be tonight."

I kept my silence, only gasping as the steward's hand became a vise and cut off my air. I writhed, trying to free myself, but my bonds prevented it. The night began to press against my eyes, and there was a strange rushing sound in my ears.

"Release her," I heard my master say, his voice sounding far away. "I am not a cruel man. You have only to tell me what you have done, and where Lappidoth is, and you will not be punished for your crime. In fact, I will reward you. I will move you up to the house, and you can work in the kitchen."

Ybyon's mouth stretched wide as he said this. I had never seen my master smile at me, so it seemed a ghastly thing to appear on his face.

"She would stuff herself until she burst," Hlagor muttered. "They all do."

"No, I think she would be careful with my stores," Ybyon said. "You would like working in the kitchen, wouldn't you, girl?"

I would. Although some of the kitchen slaves had been unkind, Seres had treated me fairly, and I thought it would not be a hardship serving under his direction. House slaves were worked hard, but they were also fed well. I would not be given overmuch, but I would never be cold or go hungry again.

This seductive offer from my master was another bowl of honey, tipped into my hands—but if I tasted of it, Jeth would die. For his sake, I kept my silence.

He motioned to Hlagor, who dragged me over to the side of the wagon. Then Ybyon cupped my chin with his hand.

"Your mother once used her sight for me," Ybyon said. "She foresaw my buying a herd of sheep, but they were diseased, and would have spread their sickness to the rest of the animals on the farm. I heeded her warning and did not buy them. Another farmer in Hatala did, and suffered the losses she had predicted. Of course, her gift belonged to me, as she did. As you do. Only you use your foresight to warn my enemy."

I shook my head, trying not to feel his touch, trying not to fall into a waking dream. "I knew of your intentions only because I overheard you speaking to Adon Hlagor about the Hebrew merchant," I said, for that, too, was the truth.

"You are my property," Ybyon said, very insistent now. "All that is yours is mine. Your thoughts, your foresight, all of it. Now, tell me what you see."

I said nothing, for I saw what he had done to my mother.

My master struck me in the face with his fist, knocking me down again. I could not control my fall, and my head landed heavily against the wood. I almost slipped into the darkness pressing around me, but I knew my life would end soon enough. I wanted to be awake for every moment left to me.

A rough hand stuffed the rag back into my mouth.

"Take her back," I heard Ybyon say. "I must make arrangements for tomorrow."

"Why not cut her throat and dump her here?" Hlagor demanded. "It will save burying the body, and give me another chance to find the Hebrew again."

"No, she warned him well enough to scare him away from you; if he is wise, he will stay out of sight until the morning. He did not strike me as a stupid man." My master turned away. "When you get to the farm, take her and lock her in the fleece shed. I will decide tomorrow how she dies."

My furtive trip to Hazor from the farm had seemed to take weeks, but the ride back lasted only a few minutes. I lay bound and helpless behind Hlagor, ignoring the jolts and bumps as I stared up at the night sky, and tried to accept what had happened to me.

All that is yours is mine. Your thoughts, your foresight, all of it.

My master had terrified me since I was first old enough to witness his capacity for cruelty, but his words betrayed his ignorance. He knew nothing about being a slave. He owned our bodies and directed our labors, and he decided how much we lived, slept, ate, and worked. That was his right, but that was all. That he believed he had the right to our souls made him seem greedy and ridiculous—a spoiled child. No one could own the thoughts and feelings of another. No one could call another's gift of sight property.

Was this why my mother had not fought harder for her life, the day when Ybyon had killed her? Had she finally seen him for what he was?

I had been told that my master had killed my mother, but no one would speak of the reasons for it. Now, after enduring his touch, I knew what had happened.

That ten sheep had died in the sickness pen overnight had not been Dasah's fault, for they carried an uncommon kind of worms that killed swiftly. She and the other slaves had separated them from the flock, expecting them to die. The master had called her from the barn, and shown her the carcasses, and demanded to know why they were dead.

I could see her calm face through his eyes, and the straightness of her back as she answered: *They were too weak to be put to graze on well-used pasture.*

Ybyon became quiet, and asked her if more animals would die, and how many he would lose. When my mother shrugged, he struck her, and dragged her over among the dead sheep. Dasah made no sound when he threw her upon the carcasses, or when he drew his knife.

Tell me what the worm sickness would do to my flocks, the master demanded.

My mother told him the truth. *They will end in the same place as the owner of the pasture upon which they graze.*

Hearing for myself her last words made my stomach heave, and I swallowed burning bile.

I had been there, as well, little more than a toddler, following my mother when Ybyon had called her. I had stood by the gate of the pen, watching. The master had shown me to myself as he looked up just before he seized my mother by her hair and jerked back her head, putting his blade to her throat.

Dasah's gaze met mine, and a sad, gentle smile curved her lips.

Tarn picked me up from the ground and clamped a hand over my mouth, so that the master did not hear my wordless screams as he pulled the blade from right to left. Through streaming tears I once more watched my mother's blood gush onto the muddy ground. Tarn's strong arms kept my writhing, kicking form from hurling itself over the fence to go to her.

In my dreams, my mother had always told me that we were so much more than our bodies, or what we were made to do with them. Ybyon could never own that part of us that Jehovah had created, and that would return to Jehovah when freed from the prison of our flesh. I desperately wanted to believe that was true.

Inside, we are always free, Dasah had said.

The stars, which had always seemed so cold and distant, appeared quite beautiful to me now. Like tiny fires they were, shooting off sparks of color I could just make out. I had thought them white, but there were circles around them, glittering, perfect rounds of blue, green, red, and purple. Or perhaps it was the tears in my eyes that turned the starlight into tiny rainbow rings. I wondered if tomorrow night my soul would be up there in the heavens, wandering about those points of light.

Do not fear death, my mother had said to me in my dreams. *It will be like sleeping, but a peaceful slumber, not one filled with the torment of visions that we suffer as living beings. No, daughter, death will be an endless night of no dreams, spent cradled in the*

*arms of one you have loved, one who went
to Jehovah's kingdom of heaven before you,
and even now waits for you to join them.*

I did not think I was afraid of dying anymore. Everyone died. The only one who had
ever loved me had been Dasah, so if she
were right, I would see her very soon. Jeth,
too, would have someone he had loved.
Whoever it was, I hoped they had to wait for
a very long time to embrace him.

"Get up."

The wagon had stopped, and Hlagor
reached over and prodded me. I struggled to
get my knees under me, but I took too long,
and he swore as he dragged me by a handful of my kesut off the wagon bed and onto
my bound ankles.

The dark fleece shed stood just beyond
the wagon.

"Your mother should have seen for me,"
the steward complained as he tossed me
over his shoulder. The master must have
beaten him badly, for he winced or groaned
with every moment. "I would have taken her
to wife. He owed me that much."

If I had wished to answer him, the rag prevented it. But I had nothing to say to Hlagor.
He was as blindly evil as my master, or per-

haps worse, for unlike Ybyon, he had no reason to despise Hebrews.

He stopped suddenly and put me down, holding me by the arm while he pulled the rag from my mouth.

"I know you are a witch. You will speak now or I will use my fists on you." He did not wait for an agreement from me. "When will the master keep his vow to me? Soon? How many sheep will he give me?"

I had no desire to summon a waking dream for one such as Hlagor, but his words acted like a spell. A vision of a storm filled my eyes from within, and a voice that was not my own began to speak of what I was seeing.

"There will be no sheep, no fortune, no wife, no children," I heard this low, terrible voice say. "You will have only your master's lies, until you speak the truth before the king."

"King Jabin?" He cuffed me with his fist. "You are mad. A king would never listen to a common slave."

Even with my ears ringing from the hard blow, I saw his death, and the voice came from me again. "Jabin will listen, but that truth will not save you, nor will the king's iron. At the mountain, you will run. Among the many, you will die alone. Where there is no water, you will drown."

Hlagor stared down at me, his face a pale smear against the black night. "Even Dasah did not dare curse me," he whispered.

"The lives you have taken have cursed you, son of Tamur," I said before the vision dimmed, and the strength went out of my limbs. My body sagged between his hands.

Hlagor dragged me over the ground and into the cold, dark fleece shed, where he dropped me like a sack of feed. He stood over me for a long moment, a silver blade in his fist.

"I should kill you," he said, his voice trembling. "It is not a difficult thing, you know. I have done it a dozen times. I can tell the master you seized my knife and plunged it into your own heart."

"With my hands bound behind my back as they are?" I gazed up at him, unsure of why I was taunting him so openly but not caring. "Better to untie me first, or make a better lie. Tell him that I stumbled and fell on it. He might actually believe you."

"You smirk at me now, when tomorrow he will have me tie you to the standing stones."

He put the blade back in the leather sheath tied to his hagora. "I will ask the master to give me the whip, and let me beat you. I will remove the skin from your back one strip at a time. Then we will see how you laugh, witch."

"You have done most of his killing for him," I reminded him. "How much longer do you think he will permit you to live, steward?"

Hlagor walked out of the fleece shed and slammed the door, bolting it from the outside. I could not see anything until my eyes adjusted to the lack of light, and then I inched my way over to a pile of shorn, uncarded bundles of wool. They had not been washed, but they would keep me warm, and I squirmed under them. As I grew warmer, my shivering ceased. All there was to see inside the shed was the rough wood-planked walls and the dirt floor, but the familiar smell of sheep comforted me.

Now all I need do was make my peace with God, for in the morning, I would die.

CHAPTER
9

"Deborah," someone whispered urgently.

I lifted my head and saw a bright eye looking through a knothole in one of the wall planks. "Go back to the barn, Meji," I whispered back. "Hlagor may be watching."

"He took the wagon and rode out of here as though chased by wolves." The wooden bar bolting the door lifted, and my friend came inside and knelt down beside me. He began working at the knots of my bonds. "You were caught in town."

"Yes." I grimaced as the cords around my wrists tightened briefly. "By the master himself."

Meji shook his head and tugged the cord from my arms, and then he went to work on my ankles. "What of the Hebrew merchant?"

"I found Jeth in time to warn him. He has taken sanctuary with a scribe who was kind enough to help me." I rubbed my sore wrists. "Go, now, and tell Tarn and the others to be careful tomorrow. The master is very angry, and you know how he takes out his temper on everyone."

He removed the cord from my ankles. "Ybyon will kill you for this." He threw the cord across the shed.

I had never seen Meji so upset. "Do not be angry, my friend. It is the last time he will hurt me, and I am glad of it. By tomorrow night I will be with Dasah again, in the kingdom of heaven." I was not sure of that, but I desperately wished it to be true.

"Did you not see this happening?" Meji demanded. "What good is this gift of yours if it costs you your life?"

"I could do nothing else. Jehovah expects much of us, but my sacrifice was not made in vain. I saved a man's *life*." I smiled, thinking of Jeth. "A good man, I think."

"Yes, a good and *rich* man. What will this Lappidoth do, once he leaves Hazor? Re-

turn to Ephraim, and live surrounded by luxuries until he is ancient and dies a painless
death." Meji made a disgusted sound. "It is
not right."

I sighed as I reached down to rub my fingers against my ankles. "It is as it is." I thought
about telling Meji of Jeth's offer to take me
with him—that way, he would know the merchant was not so selfish as he thought. But
Meji would be furious with me for not seizing
the chance to escape. A sound from outside
the shed made me go still—the heavy scrape
and thud of wood against wood—and then
the slide of footsteps through the grass.

I scrambled to the door, but it was too late.
Someone had dropped the bar into the bolt
slots, trapping Meji inside the shed with me.

The shed defeated every attempt we
made to find a way out of it. Its walls were
too thick, and the dirt floor beneath them too
hard-packed to dig out with our hands. The
bolt rendered the door immovable.

"Someone must have seen you come
here." I gave up and sat beside the pile of
fleeces. "You said you saw Hlagor driving
away? Could he have noticed you and come
back?"

"He looked to be in a rage," Meji said. "I do not think he would have seen an ox if it had crossed his path."

I stared at the wool beside me. "When the master comes for me in the morning, you will hide under the wool."

He drew back, indignant. "I shall not."

"Listen to me," I snapped. "If you think the master will delight in finding you here, you are right. It will make him very happy. For him, real joy is having reason to beat to death *two* Hebrew slaves."

"So I should hide like a coward in here and starve slowly?" He snorted. "I would rather it be quick."

I ignored that. "I will find a way to make Tarn know you are trapped in here. No one will be watching the shed after the master finishes with me. By nightfall tomorrow, Tarn will likely free you." Absently I reached up to brush the sticky fringe of hair back from my brow.

"Unless the one who dropped the bolt betrays me," Meji reminded me, his tone curiously one of satisfaction. "Then I think the master will have his great delight."

Weariness devoured my desire to stay awake on this, the last night of my life, and I lay back on the wool. "I am tired and cold. Come here and sleep with me."

"You are too restless," he said, crouching down beside me to tickle my toes. "And your feet are as two lumps of ice."

I held out my arms. "Then hold me still, and warm me."

Meji crawled into the nest of fleeces and wedged himself against my back. His arm went around my waist, and I felt his chin touch the curve of my shoulder. "When you go to sleep, do you fear the dreams?"

I shook my head and snuggled against him. "They are part of me, like my legs or my hands. How could I fear that?" It was almost true.

"Easily." He shifted, and kissed my shoulder. "If we are to die together tomorrow, it seems right that we have this last night in each other's arms."

I turned so that I faced him. Meji was not handsome, but his smile lit up his countenance the way the sun filled the sky on a cloudless day. I cared deeply for him, but he had never touched my heart.

Even on this, our last night, I could not deceive him. "You are my good friend, and I care for you and would make you happy, but . . ."

He pressed his fingers to my lips. "I know how you think of me, Deborah. I—"

Whatever he had meant to say was lost as the bolt outside was removed and the shed door flung open. Quickly I pushed some fleeces atop my friend to cover him before looking over. I expected to see Hlagor or the master stride in, but it was a woman who stepped over the threshold.

"Let him up, stable girl," she snapped, coming to stand over me. "You may die in the morning, but he will live, no thanks to you."

Meji pulled away the wool covering his face. The sight of the kitchen wench made him groan. "Not you again."

"I could not leave you here." The woman's voice became wheedling as she held out her hand to Meji. "Come. Everyone sleeps now, so it is safe. I have brought food from the master's kitchen for you. More of the cheese that you liked so much."

I frowned. So he *had* been telling the truth when he said he hadn't stolen it from Seres.

"No." Meji leaned back and put an arm around me. He looked rather defiant. "I will stay here the night with Deborah."

The kitchen wench didn't like hearing that.

"They find you here with her, you will be tied up and whipped beside her."

He moved his shoulders. "It matters not."

"Please. Whoever locked you in with her will return soon and punish both of us." Her words did not move Meji, and tears began rolling down her plump cheeks. "I beg you, do not do this. You do not have to love me, but do not waste your life on her. She is not worthy of you."

From her tone, it seemed that she thought no one was.

That explained her sneaking food to Meji, and her enjoyment in tormenting me. This woman was in love with my friend, who was indifferent to her—or was he?

I reached out and grasped the other woman's wrist, ignoring how she tried to wriggle out of my hold. The waking dream slipped over me, a veil of fine silk.

"Wadina, daughter of a trader from the north and his favorite concubine," I murmured. "You saw Meji cross from the barn to the shed. You bolted the door only to frighten him, so that he might have cause to be grateful to you when you released him. You wish me dead so I will not stand between you."

"A generous love you have, Wadina," Meji sneered, "that you would see my best friend dead."

She reacted to his words as if he had slapped her. "You cannot believe her. She lies!"

"Deborah is a truth-seer," my friend said, completely disgusted now. "Jehovah has made her so that she is incapable of lying."

I released the woman's wrist and moved away from Meji. "Go with her," I told him.

"And leave you here to face the morning alone?" His mouth became a thin, hard line. "No, Deborah."

"I saw you with this one," I told him, nodding toward Wadina. "In a field of wheat. It was near a simple farmhouse, in the mountains beyond the lake. You were plowing the soil, and she carried your son on her hip. There were flowers, and a little girl child picking them. A child with her hair and your smile." I would not feel envy. I would not. "You must go with her. She is your freedom, and your destiny."

"A son? A daughter? A farm?" Overcome, Wadina covered her face with her hands and wept again.

"How can I have children with such a

soggy female?" Meji complained. "I do not even *like* her. And we will never be free. I told you: I will not have children born only to be sent to the auction block."

The kitchen wench wailed and ran from the shed.

"You will be freed, very soon," I promised, my eyelids drooping. "Go now. She loves you, and will make a fine mother to your children."

"I cannot leave you like this."

I did not wish to tell him what else I had seen in the vision, but it was the only way to make him go. "If you do not, and you are found here in the morning, those children will never be born. The master will kill you."

"How can you say such things to me?" He sounded appalled.

"Because they are the truth," I mumbled. "As you well know."

"Deborah—no, do not sleep—I will go, but you must come with me." He shook my shoulder.

Tarn appeared in the open doorway. "Meji. Come away now."

I might go with them and flee into the city, but Ybyon would know someone had released me, and every slave on the farm would be punished for my escape.

"Go with him," I mumbled, "and do not waste the gifts Jehovah offers you."

Tarn came over and pulled Meji away from me. I snuggled down into the fleece, sighed, and fell asleep.

I sat on the edge of the ivory stone fountain, looking down at a ghostly reflection. The water was as flat and lovely as the gleam of light on silver, and I could see the face perfectly. I did not wish to look at it, or to be here. I wanted only to sleep. Could I not have one night without the dreams?

"For the work to be done, your heart must be open to God, Deborah," a sweet, low voice said. It was coming from the water in the fountain.

I looked down at the reflection. If not for the eyes, I would have thought it the image of my mother, Dasah. But no—the woman in the water was me.

I had never looked so strange to myself. My hair fell around the face in soft waves, but it was much longer and cleaner than I had ever worn it. There was a strange scar on my face, as well: a dark patch in the shape of a crescent moon.

I lifted my fingers to touch the mark, but

could not feel it. I ran my palm over my hair and felt the stickiness of my cinder-and-fat dye.

"Fear not what your eyes tell you," the reflection said. "For we are one and the same soul."

I wanted to get up from the fountain and run away. Instead, I watched my red, work-callused hand reach out toward the water. The reflection lifted her smooth white hand as if to take mine. Around the base of her fingers were narrow bands of silver, one studded with two dark red stones. A finely worked chain of copper glittered around her thin wrist.

"Why do you come here?" I demanded, snatching my hand back. "What do you want from me?"

"You bring others to drink from the fountain of God, yet you go thirsty." She smiled, as if this amused her. "Why have you never sought a vision of your own future, daughter of Dasah?"

"It is forbidden." I turned away from the reflection, feeling sick. Now the storm would come, and all would be dark and frightening. To my surprise, the sun still scattered buttery yellow light through the thick green leaves, and the birds continued to sing. I rose and looked around me. "Heavenly Father, tell me what I must do."

"Deborah."

The voice was Jeth's, and he was somewhere close to me, but I could not see him. Tears of anger burned my eyes. I knew I would never see him again, but to be denied his memory here, in this place . . .

"You must believe in the Lord God's love," Jeth said. "Trust in Him above all others, and He will fill your eyes with wonders."

"I do not want wonders. I only wanted—" Furious and wretched, I fell down onto the ground and beat my fists into the rich soil. "Yes, I wanted more. I wanted you. I wanted my mother, here, alive. I wanted freedom from Ybyon. I have none of it. I have nothing. *I die with nothing.*"

I had screamed the words, releasing them like vile fluid from a festering wound. As they left me, I felt my heart go still, and then cool, gentle hands touched my face. I was embraced, held like a child, my cheek touching against a soft shoulder.

I looked up into Dasah's eyes. "Mother." I felt horribly guilty, behaving like a shrieking, ungrateful brat in her presence. "Forgive me."

"Shhh." She cradled me in her arms. "There is nothing to forgive. You have carried your burden alone too long."

We sat thus in silence for a long time, and I would have happily done so forever.

"Do you remember how the little newborn lamb bleated when you took him from his mother?" Dasah asked softly. "After the master struck her down?"

How could I forget those frightened, plaintive cries? "Yes."

"Such cruelty, such a terrible parting, and yet the lamb thrives, and the ewe, even though she was separated from him, provides nourishment for him." She tilted my chin to make me look up at her. "Why do you think that is, Deborah?"

"I rubbed him with her birth water."

Dasah laughed. "Yes. You did. Perhaps I should try the same." She reached into the fountain, scooping up a handful of water, and poured it over my scalp. It felt so cool and clean as it ran through my hair. "You are my beautiful child. The moment you came into the world was the greatest blessing of my life. What joy you brought me, Deborah. What joy."

Her words did not make me feel the same.

They tore at me as cruelly as if she had shouted hatred of me. "I am not a lamb," I whispered. "I never knew you. We shall never be together again." I wished there were such things as curses, for I would have put one on my master for taking Dasah from me.

"We are together now." My mother anointed me with a second handful of water. "With nothing but our souls do we come into the world, and with nothing but our souls do we leave. It is the will of Jehovah, my daughter. Do you know why that is?"

The sunlight filled my eyes, and something warm and wonderful entered my heart. "Only our souls can make the journey. Nothing else may go."

"Yes." She pressed her lips to my brow. "Jehovah has granted you the power to see the future, and the strength to carry the burden of speaking only truth. When it is your time, He will welcome you into the kingdom of heaven, and I will be waiting for you there. But your earthly journey is not yet come to an end."

"It will tomorrow," I told her.

"Perhaps." She brought a cupped hand to my lips, and I drank from it. The water was softer and sweeter than honey. When her hand was empty, she kissed my brow a second time. "I loved you from the moment you were put into my arms. You were so little but perfectly made, and such a good baby." Her eyes glistened. "How I have missed you. How I have wanted you back in my arms."

"Mother." I buried my face against her breast and wept like a lost lamb.

CHAPTER
10

They came for me in the gray light before
the sun rose, and dragged me from my bed
of fleece. Neither of the master's guards
seemed surprised that the cords from my
wrists and ankles lay on the ground, but retrieved one length and tied my hands before
me. They moved quickly but with the reluc-
tance of those who did not relish their tasks.

I saw what the master had planned for me
as soon as I was pushed out of the shed. Instead of the stone massebot to which Ybyon
preferred to tie slaves for punishment, two
long, thick pit stakes had been hammered

into the ground on either side of one of the terebinth trees that surrounded the slaves' privy. There were short ropes tied to the stakes, and these had been fashioned into loops.

I did not see Hlagor waiting for me, but the master was there, as were all the other slaves and shepherds. Guards armed with spears and knives stood before them, and Seres stood off to one side, a coiled ox whip in his hand.

"Bring her forth." My master sat on a decorated chair someone had brought down from the main house. His robes were the finest I had ever seen him wear, and he sipped wine from a bronze goblet. As if this were all some sort of entertainment being put on for his pleasure.

Perhaps that was all I was.

The guards escorted me to stand before the master, who waved his goblet. "Put her on her knees so that she may entreat me to spare her."

I lifted my chin. "I shall not beg for my life, Adon."

He seemed startled. "Did you learn nothing from your mother, girl?"

"I learned much before you killed her," I said, not taking my eyes from his. "She did not fear death, and neither shall I."

"Then you are as foolish as she was." Ybyon motioned with one hand. "Put her to the tree, then. The lash will sweeten her tongue."

I did not resist as the guards guided me over to the tree. I faced the rough bark and held out my hands so that they could be tied by the wrists to the pit stakes. The wooden rods were just far enough apart to stretch out my arms.

"Deborah." It was Seres's voice, coming from just behind me. "The master has ordered me do this thing. I will make it as quick as I can, but . . ."

I understood. Beating to death a young woman, even one as thin and undernourished as I was, would take some time and effort. "I am sorry that this task was put on you, Seres. It should be Hlagor's lot."

"He ran off last night. I hope I am chosen for his turn at the post, for that one I would enjoy slicing to pieces one lash at a time." The kitchen master hesitated, and then said, "What I do here this morning, girl, is not of my choosing. I would have it any other way. They say you cannot lie, is this so?" I nodded. "When you go before the Gods of the afterlife, will you . . . speak well of me?"

"I do not believe in your gods." I leaned my head against the rough bark of the tree. "But in truth I hold no animosity toward you for this, Seres."

He thanked me and stepped back. One of the guards tore the kesut from my shoulders, and rent the fabric beneath until I felt the damp, cold morning air on the skin of my back.

"Deborah, daughter of the slave woman Dasah, broke the law and ran away last night," I heard the master say. "She knew she was forbidden to leave the farm, but to spite me she escaped. In town she conspired with a dishonest merchant to cheat me out of full payment for a debt. The Gods smiled upon me, however, and led me to discover her plotting. I caught her in Hazor last night and brought her back here to face just punishment."

No one made a sound. I turned my head, resting my cheek against the tree trunk so I could see the master's face. He looked almost pleased, but I felt a surge of sadness. How horrifying, to be so perverse as to feel pleasure only by causing others pain.

"I am troubled by this incident," Ybyon said, belying his happy expression. "By her actions, and the silence of those who should have told me that she had fled the farm, I am within my rights to punish all the barn stable slaves."

I heard the hiss of braided leather some feet away from me.

My master waited several moments before he spoke again—probably to relish the fear on the gaunt faces around him—and then he said, "I have decided to be generous. No one but this ungrateful, evil girl will be whipped. I will not hold back food from your mouths."

My hands uncurled, and I went limp against the tree, such was my relief. *He will not starve them more. They will be given enough to go on.*

"But remember what you see done here today," Ybyon continued. "If another of you ever attempts to escape your duties to me, I will have every slave on this farm tied up and given thirty lashes."

Seres muttered something that sounded

ugly, too soft for the master to hear. That gave me some hope that he might show more sympathy toward the slaves. They would need someone like him after I was gone.

Another hiss came, much louder, as the whip divided the air. I was going to die now, and to my shame I was shaking. *He promised to make it quick. Jehovah, give me strength.* I tried to summon the image of Dasah's face, and the love in my dream-mother's eyes, and braced myself.

Bright, hot pain slashed across me from shoulder to hip, and I jerked, surprised at how much it hurt.

"One," Seres called out.

It seemed only a heartbeat before the whip struck me again. It seemed to hardly touch me; then the pain exploded as the knotted hide slithered off my flesh. I shook all over, and my brow scraped against the tree bark.

"Two."

I bit my lip, determined not to scream. *Take me soon, Heavenly Father,* I prayed to Jehovah. *Let me see my mother waiting for me with her arms—*

"Three."

My back became a web of fire, and I would have fallen but for the ropes around my wrists. Somehow I kept my feet under me, but I could not rest my full weight against the tree to be ready for the next.

"Four."

The whip caught my braid and jerked my head back. My chin bounced, and my teeth slammed together as Seres jerked it loose and lashed me again, this time slicing my back from one side of my ribs to the other. Dimly I felt something warm and wet trickling down my back and between my legs as the whip drew blood and I let go my water.

"Five."

Seres was too quick; I was still writhing from the last blow when the next landed. A cry spilled from my throat as the stretched muscles of my arms and back cramped and spasmed under the agony left behind by the heavy lashes.

Panting through the pain, I turned my head and saw the master had moved his chair closer, so that he sat only a few feet away from the tree. Ybyon did not take his eyes off me as he handed his goblet to the servant hovering behind him. "More wine."

How could he sit there and watch this? How could anyone hate so much?

The whip hissed again, and something cut into my cheek as the force of the blow drove me against the tree. My knees buckled, and the ropes bit into my wrists like hungry rats. I could not stand, I could not fall. I was not sure how much more I could take without screaming.

"Six."

I screamed. The bitter wine of blood and tears flooded my mouth, and as I tried to breathe, I discovered there was no more air. My face was bleeding from scraping against the tree's rough trunk, and the ropes were eating into my flesh. The tree and the whip were going to grind me slowly between them.

"Seven."

It was too much. The world became the end of a branding iron, and I could not see the master or even the tree anymore. Beyond the buzzing sound in my ears, I heard men's voices, and an angry shout, but I did not care. I waited for the next blow, sure this one would kill me, but it did not come.

Why does he not hit me? My thoughts felt

thick and useless, like the blood on my tongue. *He promised. He promised.*

"Cut her down."

The rats at my wrists ceased gnawing, but I could not see clearly to thank whoever had chased them away. I tried to fall to the ground so that I could die, but there were hands, and they would not let me.

"Deborah."

Something light and soft touched my back, but even that was too much, and I cried out. The same softness moved over my face, caressing and gentle.

"Look at me, please, Deborah."

I would have ignored the voice and slipped into the waiting darkness, only it belonged to Jeth, and surely he could not be here. I forced my eyes open to see his face close to mine. In his hand was a blood-stained cloth, which he used to wipe my mouth and chin.

The blood was mine, but I did not care. I could not believe he was here, where the master could do whatever he wished to him. I made my mouth move. "You . . . should be . . . hiding."

"She needs a healer," Jeth said to someone nearby before he looked down at me. "I knew I should have come for you last night. Forgive me for not preventing this."

"Whatever this Hebrew has told you is a lie," my master's voice said close by. "His sheep will be delivered as we agreed. I am outraged that you would come here to question me. Do you not know who I am?"

"We know you well enough, sheepherder," a strange voice said. "What about the girl? Why do you have her beaten?"

"She is a slave, and she ran away," Ybyon replied. "As her owner, I have the right to punish her for such. She is my property."

"Tell them why she ran away," Jeth said as he lifted me carefully into his arms. "Tell them how she came to town to warn me of your plot to have another of your slaves kill me for my silver."

Murmurs swept through those around us. I was able to see better now, but I could not make sense of it. Why were the king's guards here? They never came to the farm.

My master laughed. "You Hebrews think the world wishes you dead. Well, I wished only to sell you some sheep. That is not a crime."

Beyond Ybyon and the guards surrounding him, the slaves stood clustered together, watching everything. They parted as a man walked through them and toward us.

"My master does not speak the truth," Hlagor said. "I will offer sworn witness against him."

I saw Ybyon go very still. "You have no business speaking to my visitors, steward. Return to the house."

"No." Hlagor stopped and pointed at the master. "The Hebrew has spoken the truth. Adon Ybyon sent me to town to find the Hebrew last night. He gave me herbs to drug him—"

"Silence," my master hissed. "Not another word, or I will have your head."

One of the king's guard lifted his long hereb, as if he meant to do as Ybyon threatened and strike the steward. "You speak against your own master?"

"If I do not, he will have me killed to conceal his crimes," Hlagor said. "I am a slave. I had no choice but to follow his orders. Ybyon wished to cheat this Hebrew, and see him dead. He despises his kind, and told me to kill him."

My master took a step toward the steward, his hands knotted into fists. "You lie. I know nothing of what you plotted. Whatever you did in town last night was of your own accord, not mine."

"If you know nothing of his acts," another of the guards demanded, "then how do you know he was in town last night?"

My master's mouth worked for a moment. "I gave him permission to go. It does not prove I knew what he intended to do to this poor merchant."

The king's men regarded the steward, and the oldest said, "How can you prove what you say, slave?"

"The Hebrew was not the first man my master wanted dead," Hlagor said. He did not sound the least frightened, and glared at Ybyon with open hatred. "There were many others, some wealthy traders from cities to the east and south. I killed them and put them in the river. The master took all their silver and animals for himself—"

Ybyon shouted and rushed at the steward, but two of the guards caught him and held him. He cursed and struggled between them. "He is a slave. He lies. I have had no one killed. Whatever he did was none of my doing, do you hear? He is a lying, murdering slave who should be executed right here for daring accuse me."

Tarn came forward. "A year ago the master came to wake me in the night. In his wagon were three bodies: that of a farmer who would not sell him the pastureland he wanted, as well as the farmer's wife and young child. My master had blood on his hands. They were not Hebrews. I will show you where I buried their bodies."

Ybyon stared in disbelief at the old slave. "You dare cross me."

"I know the farmer the old one speaks of," Hlagor said. "The master desired that man's land and livestock, but he would not sell. After the farmer disappeared, he sent shepherds to bring his sheep here and add them to his flocks. He also went to the magistrate and was given the land as payment for a debt that never existed."

"I will have both of you hanged from that tree for the crows to devour," my master said through his teeth.

"My old master tried to choke the life out of me." Tarn touched the mark on his throat. "He, too, failed."

I closed my eyes as the slaves began to shout, and Ybyon was dragged off by the king's guard. Whatever happened to me now, at least some justice would be taken.

PART TWO

Song of Barak

CHAPTER
11

Later I would learn that Jeth himself carried me away from the whipping tree. Time passed as I lay in darkness, until I woke in a cool, quiet place. I thought I might be in the barn until I opened my eyes and saw that I was on a blanket-covered mat, surrounded by brick walls. Someone had stripped off my clothes and draped my hips with another blanket, leaving my torn back bare. I turned my head and tensed as pain stabbed through me, and then I saw Wadina standing over me. Remembering her hatred of me, I cringed a little, but she did not strike me.

"The Hebrew merchant has gone into

town to fetch the healer," she said, and carefully put the warm, wet cloth to my bare shoulder.

"The master?" I gasped, for even the gentle pressure sent fresh arrows of agony through me.

"Taken away by the guard for more questioning, as well as Tarn and Hlagor. The entire family has gone to beseech the king for his release." She turned and brought back a cup. She lifted my head and held the brim to my lips. "Drink," she urged. "Seres prepared it. He said it will ease your pain."

I was so thirsty, I did not care if it was poison, and so I drank. The tea was flavored with strong spices and something slightly bitter, and sweetened with honey. The drink made me feel very sleepy, and as Wadina administered to me, I closed my eyes and drifted away.

How long I slept after that first waking, I could not say. Several times I roused enough to drink what was held to my lips, whether it was weak broth or more of Seres's strong tea. Damp, cool clothes regularly moved over my unmarked skin, and some sort of numbing salve was spread over my back. Sometimes I thought I heard someone speaking to me, but I was too tired to answer with more than a mumbled word. Once I was lifted into strong arms, and placed on a softer blanket.

Dawn played over my face, finally waking me, and I opened my eyes to see its pale golden light streaming in with cool air from an open window. For a moment I simply lay there and watched the sunrise, an orange-red jewel that painted the long, thin clouds on the horizon pink and gold.

I live another day.

"She wakes at last," a wry and familiar voice said. "I had thought she might hibernate until spring."

Another man laughed. "That sounds a tempting prospect."

Carefully I lifted myself onto my elbows, and my eyes followed the sound of the voices. I was astonished to see Parah and Jeth sitting on a bench by a wall decorated with fine tapestries.

"Where am I?" I grimaced at the dry sound of my voice and my own discourtesy. "Please, would you tell me?"

"The king granted me use of Ybyon's home until his judgment is passed," Jeth said, rising and coming to crouch beside the sleeping mat upon which I lay. "His family has also been arrested. I thought you should not sleep in the barn." He held out a wooden cup. "Here, drink."

Parah grinned at me before rising and leaving the room.

I recalled Wadina saying Seres had mixed something into a drink to ease my pain. "Will it make me sleep again?"

"No, it is only water." He watched as I drank, and smiled when I emptied the cup. "You are feeling better."

"Yes." I was no longer naked, but dressed in a long middo made of thin, loosely woven linen. My back pained me, but not as it had when last I spoke to Wadina. "I have been sleeping, all this time?" He nodded. "How long?"

"Since the healer came, about eight days ago," Jeth said, shocking me. "He thought you should be kept sleeping. Does your back still pain you? He has returned to town, but I can send for him again."

I moved my shoulders gingerly. The length of my back felt sore and stiff, and I could feel the itch of newly scabbed skin, but it was nothing compared with my memories of writhing under the fiery whip. My hair had been washed and brushed, however, and felt much better than it had full of Meji's thick, smelly dye.

"I do not need a healer." I wanted to ask why Parah had come, but more pressing needs made themselves known. I eyed the chamber pan nearby, but did not wish to make use of it. "Is there a privy I can use?"

Jeth helped me up from the mat and kept my arm tucked in his as he led me from the room and into another, smaller chamber.

I saw to my needs, and left the chamber to find Jeth waiting in the other room. "I saw Parah. Where did he go? And what did you mean about judgment—who is being judged? Did the king's men allow Tarn to return? Has Hlagor been imprisoned?"

His teeth flashed white against his short beard as he laughed. "You would have me answer all of that at the same time?"

"I have been sleeping for eight days," I reminded him, and then went to sit on the bench because my legs were not yet so steady. "In the master's house, which I would not believe myself, if I did not see it around me with my own eyes."

His smile turned grim for a moment. "You should be given this house as his punishment for the abuse he inflicted on you."

I shook my head. "Even if it were to come to pass, a slave cannot hold or own property."

He came and sat down beside me. "I have no right to be angry when it is you who have suffered so much. It is just that you were so weak when I brought you here, and I feared the wounds would fester and fever would take you."

"I am still alive." But for how much longer? "Were any of the other slaves punished in my place?"

"No, they are all well, and being cared for. Ybyon and his family remain in town, under close guard. Tarn led the king's men to where the bodies of those your master killed lay buried."

"So he spoke the truth." I had wondered if it were so.

He looked sad and disgusted. "One of the other farmers was able to identify the man by a protective amulet he wore under his clothing. Today Ybyon will be judged for that crime, as well as several others, before the town magistrates and the merchant guild of Hazor. They might not care that he tried to cheat a Hebrew out of silver and sheep, but the man he killed was the cousin of a powerful advisor at the king's court."

"What of Hlagor?"

"The king has exonerated him," Jeth said, shaking his head. "But I am sure it is because he stands as witness against Ybyon."

I thought of my vision of his future. "His time will come." I looked up as Parah came into the room. "Adon, I thank you for helping Adon Lappidoth."

"He is a very troublesome houseguest," Parah assured me. "Now, you must be hungry. I know I would be if all I had for eight days were a few bowls of watery broth. Shall we dine together?"

"I cannot eat here." When his face went blank, I added, "I must return to my place in the barn. I will eat with the others."

"That is completely ridiculous." Parah seized my arm and helped me up from the bench. "You will eat with me and Jeth, and we will entertain you with tales of our daring as we rushed here to rescue you and have your master chained like the mad dog he is. Men as brave as we deserve a chance to boast of our heroism."

I went along with them to the kitchen, where Seres was directing the women to set bowls and platters on the family table. He barely glanced up from his own work carving a large chunk of mutton roasted with herbs, but said, "Sit down. Wadina, bring the men something to drink. That fresh milk will do for Deborah."

I sat on the long bench seat that had only ever been occupied by my master and his family. Despite the many delicious-looking dishes crowding the surface of the table, I could not relax. I dared not touch anything.

"It is only food," Parah said from across the table. "I am sure the cook has killed everything properly." He gave Wadina a serene smile as she brought him wine. "This time."

Seres put a bowl of soup thick with beans and herbs before me. "You may be able to scribble words on parchment, but you know nothing about properly preparing meat," he growled at the scribe. "Rare mutton is more tender and flavorful than overcooked mutton."

"Tender indeed," Parah pretended to whisper to me, "for when I pierced last night's mutton with my fork, it baaed, got up, and walked off the table."

Jeth chuckled, and I could not help my own smile. Satisfied at having needled Seres and amused me, Parah broke off a chunk from a round lehem and used it to fish some beans from his broth, while Wadina poured wine for Jeth and gave me a cup filled to the brim with fresh, cool milk.

I looked down at the steaming bowl Seres had placed before me and swallowed. Hunger made my stomach clench, but I was sitting at the master's table, and I had never eaten among anyone but other slaves. We were not given our own bowls or permitted cups. I did not know what to do with my hands.

"Is the soup too hot?" Jeth asked. "Would you prefer something else?"

I stared at him. "No, it is fine." There was more food on the table than I had ever been near, and I would eat a little of it without going at it like a hungry dog. Then I saw Jeth carefully cradle his bowl between his hands and blow a breath across the surface of the broth before sipping from the edge.

I picked up my bowl and did exactly as he. The hot soup burned my lips and tongue, but it tasted so marvelous that I didn't care. The strange, savory taste of the herbs enlivened the blandness of the beans, and there were other flavors that I did not know.

Jeth put down his bowl and took up a piece of bread, and like Parah used it to take beans from the broth. I put down my soup and reached out for a round lehem sitting on a plate near my hand.

"Deborah!"

I nearly knocked over my cup of milk as I jumped from the bench and assumed a humble position, bowing my head and clasping my hands.

Seres came to stand beside me. "Must you scare the very life out of her, old man?"

I looked up and sighed. "Tarn." His face and garments were so clean that I hardly recognized him. "You are well?" Obviously he was, but my heart was pounding so that I could not think.

"Well and very pleased to see you up on your feet." He came and gave me a gentle but affectionate embrace. "Sit and eat. I did not mean to disturb your meal."

Shame made the soup I had eaten form a lump inside me. Here I was, gobbling up the best food from the master's kitchen while Tarn and the others had to make do with the stingy portion given to the farmworkers.

"Could Tarn"—I dared to address Seres directly—"share some of my soup?"

"If he is still hungry," the kitchen steward said. "All the food I sent down to the barn for

the morning meal may have filled his belly."
Of Tarn, he asked, "Did your men enjoy the
new grapes and cheese?"

"Very much." Tarn grinned. "I think
Chemesh's sickness has finally gone, thanks
to your herb tea. We had thought we might
need to build him a shelter next to the privy.
We will keep him inside for another few days,
though, as he is still weak and should rest."

I sat down, feeling very confused. Slaves
were never given much fruit, only that which
was not fit for the master's table. Never were
we given cheese or medicinal teas. Slaves
who worked the herds were not permitted to
stay inside or rest unless it was time for all of
us to sleep, and we were allowed precious
little of that.

Obviously much had been done while I
had been sleeping, but what would be the
price? When the master returned and
learned of this, he would be furious.

Tarn sat next to me and studied my incred-
ulous expression. "You look astonished, child,
but it is true. All has been much improved for
us since Adon Lappidoth came to save you."

"But cheese, Tarn?" I whispered, afraid to
say it any louder. "Seres *gives* you *cheese*?"

The old slave laughed. "Cheese, and

more good things to eat than I can count. The men are becoming so fat, they will soon be wishing to nap during the noon hour."

Knowing Ybyon as I did, I could not be amused. "Do you know how angry the master will be? When he returns and finds his stores have been shared with slaves, he will starve us for months."

"I do not think that will happen, Deborah," Parah said. "King Jabin views the murder of free Canaanites, especially innocent women and children, very seriously." He sighed. "A pity he does not feel the same about Hebrews, or your master might face true justice for causing your mother's death."

"He will do that soon enough, when he stands before Jehovah to be judged in the kingdom of heaven." So I hoped.

Jeth noticed I had stopped eating and touched my arm. "Perhaps you would care to take a walk with me? The fresh air will do you good, and there are new lambs that came while you were resting."

I nodded and rose, following him gratefully out of the kitchen. Try as I might, I could not imagine the farm without Ybyon's harsh presence. He had always been there. If he was imprisoned for the killings, who would take charge in his place? None of his family had ever shown any interest in running the farm or doing work; they were plump, pampered folk who spent so much time idling indoors that they were as pale as the strange traders who came from the far northern countries. Their pale skin would surely burn red if they stepped outside for longer than a few minutes.

Thinking of them made me consider the other slaves, who were really my only family. If the king seized the master's property, what would happen to us? Every town had an auction block for slaves at market. Would we be sold off, one by one? Would I have to learn how to please a new master? Would he be as Ybyon had been, or worse?

"Has living here been as bad for you as I have been told?" Jeth asked, startling me from my thoughts.

"I do not know what you have been told." I stopped by the lamb pen and counted ten new little ones. They were larger and healthier-looking than any I had seen, but I did not spot the small ram I had taken from the ewe the master struck just after his birth. "Do you know, have we lost any of the lambs?"

"I do not believe so. Tarn has reported every birth, and you can see for yourself how they are thriving," he said. "We are bringing their mothers to this pen each night, and three times each day, so they can have enough milk. It will help them grow into stronger animals."

That was not how the master treated lambs—more to worry about. "No wonder they are so fat. It would be wise to watch how much they nurse after the first week they are born—if they grow too heavy, they will have belly problems. The ewes, too, can become too thin from giving too much milk, or develop sores and lumps in their bags." I would have to tend to the ewes this evening and see they were not ailing.

Jeth leaned against the pen fence and regarded me. "You know a great deal about sheep."

"I have cared for this flock since I was little." I reached down to scratch beneath a fuzzy chin, and earned a low baa of delight from the lamb. "Sheep are perhaps not the cleverest of animals, and they can be stubborn, but they will show much affection to a kind hand. They play, too, as Tarn says the little children of free men do." I gave him an apologetic look. "I have never spent much time with free people."

"Why have you never married?"

The question puzzled me. "Slaves are not permitted to do so. If the master wished to breed me, he might put me with one of the men until my moon time ceased, but he has never done thus." I was glad of it, too, for I had always feared having a child. Tarn had encouraged me to make myself useful even when I was very young, so the master would not be so tempted to sell me. Like Meji, I could not bear the thought of Ybyon doing the same to a child of my body.

Jeth's brows drew together. "Surely that is not the only way it happens with slaves."

"On this farm, it is." I thought of Chemesh. "I have heard that some masters are kind and allow two slaves to live as husband and wife, but there is always the risk of one or the other being sold off to pay a debt, as Chemesh was." I told him briefly of the slave's sad history.

"That is a deplorable practice," he said, sounding angry now. "I cannot understand how you came to be here. What of your mother's people? Tarn told me she died when you were very young, but that she was not born into slavery. Did no one come to look for her? Why have you not appealed to them? Surely they would help you."

"I do not know my father's people, but Tarn said they were not Hebrews. No one will speak of it to me." I walked past the lamb pen and viewed the sheepfold, where the shepherds were untying the dogs and preparing to move the main herd out to graze. "If my mother had a tribe, they must certainly have forgotten her by now. They would not know of me."

"Do you know the name of your mother's tribe?"

I wished for once that I could lie. "She told Tarn she was of the tribe of Benjamin."

"I am of the tribe of Benjamin." Jeth stepped in front of me. "We dwell only in the mountains to the south. How did she come to be a slave in Hazor?"

"I cannot say." Tarn might know, but I did not want to force him to tell me the truth, or reveal my gift to Jeth. It was a stupid vanity, but I did not wish to see him look upon me with revulsion. While he was here, I wanted him to think me like any other woman. "I should go back to the house and change into something appropriate for working."

"Talk to me, Deborah," he said softly, insistently. "Tell me everything that you know. I must understand how a kinswoman of mine ends up a slave to a Canaanite."

I could not be like other women. I would never be. To allow him to think so was as much as lying to him, I realized, and sighed. "All I know is that my mother was a truth-seer, and she could not lie. I am the same."

He tilted his head. "A truth-seer? I have never heard of such. What does it mean?"

"Truth-seers can sometimes see what will be. We see in dreams mostly, but we can also find a truth in someone by touching them." I swallowed. "Tarn said my mother was branded with a witch's mark when she was a child, to warn others. Her people must have cast her out or sold her to slavers."

"We do not brand children," Jeth said firmly, "and we do not sell them into slavery."

"Someone did." I touched my forehead where Dasah's witch mark had been. "Ybyon killed her in front of me, when I was barely old enough to walk, but I have no memory of that."

His face paled, and his eyes turned cold. "Who cared for you after your master murdered her?"

"Tarn and the other slaves here did," I told him. "An old shepherd who died three winters past was the one who delivered me of my mother. He said I came into the world with a mask of skin over my face, but my mother said she had been born the same, and that it was the sign I would be a truth-seer."

His fierce gaze softened. "All of this, your mother murdered, and you left serving her killer." He shook his head. "What you must think of our tribe."

"It matters not." My attention was drawn to a group of three Canaanites walking down from the main house toward us. "Who are those men?"

Jeth looked over. "From the cut of their robes, deputies from the magistrate's office, I think."

"Merchant." The oldest of the deputies gestured for Jeth to come forward. "King Jabin sends us to deliver his word. Free Hebrews are no longer welcome in Hazor. You must leave before the sun sets, or you will be arrested."

CHAPTER
12

Appalled, I covered my mouth with my hand, but Jeth did not seem at all disturbed by the order.

"This is an official deportation decree from the king?" he asked the deputy, who nodded. "I would see a copy of the scroll."

The deputy exchanged glances with his two companions. "I suppose it will do no harm to show him." He removed a roll of hide from his satchel and handed it to Jeth.

I did not bother to look at the intricate marks on the scroll, for I could not read. Instead I murmured, "I will go and fetch Parah."

"That is not necessary." Jeth rolled up the

decree and handed it back to the deputy. "I will leave, but I will take the sheep that I bought from Ybyon with me. He is being judged by your magistrate today."

"That one's judgment has been delivered. You will have to speak to the magistrate about removing anything from this property, for it is to be sold off—"

"Alas, it is no longer for sale." Parah appeared beside the deputies. "One of my staff just delivered the agreement. The magistrate decided to accept my generous purchase offer." He turned to Jeth. "I am the new owner of this property, and as such, I will give you the animals which you and Ybyon agreed upon."

"I am grateful," Jeth said, although he didn't look surprised. "I would ask you for one more boon, Scribe Parah." He folded his hand around mine. "I would ask you give Deborah her freedom, so that she may come with me."

Parah gave me a long shrewd look, and then the corners of his mouth curled up. "I cannot say if she will go with you, but I will see to it that she has her freedom scroll before the hour is through."

I was going to be free?

I could not speak or think. I did not know what to do. I was going to be free. No more a slave to any man.

The sun dimmed, and the men around me spoke, but I could not hear them. I had gone deaf, and I was going blind.

I reached out to Jeth, but he was miles away. So I embraced the closest thing to me, which was the cold, hard ground.

"I do not think she hit her head," Jeth was saying to someone.

I struggled back to awareness, and found I was being carried again, this time through the barn to a pile of straw. "Jehovah save me. Am I dreaming? Did Parah say . . . No, for if I were dreaming, it would be true."

"Deborah." Jeth smiled down at me. "You fainted."

"I have the fever." I pressed a hand to my brow, but it was cool. "I must. I heard the scribe say . . ." I shook my head, too confused to go on.

"Parah is gone to write up your freedom scroll," Jeth said. He flung his cloak out over the straw before lowering me on it. "Do not be afraid. He said you may stay here and work for him as a free woman, or he will help you find a position with a good family. You will never have to beg for your bread."

The thought of no longer being a slave was too much for me to take in. I gazed up at him. "What of the king's decree? What will happen to you now?"

"That is a problem our friend the scribe cannot solve." He sighed. "I must herd my sheep to the river and leave Hazor by nightfall, or my property will be seized by the king's men and I will be imprisoned."

"You must not waste another moment here." I struggled to my feet. "I will ask Tarn and the others to help you move the herd. We have shepherds who are experienced drovers, and I am sure Parah will give them leave. I—" I stopped as I recalled what else he had said to the scribe. "Did you . . . Did you say before that you wished me to come with you?"

He nodded. "I would, very much. It is the sensible thing to do, you know. The king's deportation decree specifies all free Hebrews, which you will be as soon as the ink dries on your freedom scroll. I think Parah will do his best to protect you, and you might pass as a Canaanite woman, but you will always risk being arrested. As your kinsman, I consider it my responsibility to reunite you with your mother's tribe."

I did not particularly care about my mother's tribe, and there were other risks beyond exposure. "What of Ybyon?" My master would seek revenge for losing his farm to Parah; of that I had no doubt.

"The farmer Ybyon killed was a favorite of the king's adviser. The adviser took personal interest in seeing that the magistrate's judgment was as severe as the law permits. Your master and his family will share the same fate as his property. They are to be sold on the block before the new moon." From his tone, Jeth didn't seem to think that was enough punishment.

As much as I disliked my former master, it was not difficult to pity him now. He would never wear the yoke of slavery lightly, or spend a day not thinking of how it came to be on his shoulders.

"What this will do to his family. He cared for them so that they never had to work. The children." I closed my eyes for a moment, sickened.

"They all profited from his greed," Jeth said, "so the magistrate declared they would share in this, as well."

We both sat in silence, contemplating Ybyon's fate.

"Are you satisfied with the judgment, Deborah?" When I glanced at him, he added, "Ybyon did kill your mother, and he will never be made to answer for that."

"He will someday, when his earthly life ends," I assured him. "Until then, he will endure some of the same suffering he inflicted on his own slaves. It is the sort of punishment Jehovah might give." And now I wondered if the One and True God had guided events so that this would come to pass.

"You do not rejoice in his downfall," Jeth murmured.

I had never forgiven my master for taking my mother away from me when I needed her most, or for the evil and cruelty he had inflicted on so many others. But I could not take pleasure from knowing he would suffer.

"I cannot," I said slowly. "It would make me as he is, and I would rather forgive him than allow his hatred to poison my heart."

Jeth covered my hand with his. "Will you come with me to Ephraim, Deborah?" Before I could answer, he added, "It will be a long journey downriver, and I know that you are still weak, but I will make you comfortable, and look after you. That is the way of our tribe."

I wished to ask him a dozen questions, but there was no time for that. Nor could I summon a waking dream to see what the future held; the future had grown past all my hopes.

It was almost a blessing when Meji stepped out of the shadows of a stall near us. His eyes were glittering, and I could almost feel the silent anger making his shoulders so rigid. Apparently he had heard every word Jeth and I had said.

I withdrew my hand from Jeth's gentle grip. "May I have a few moments to speak with my friend?"

Jeth gave Meji a long look before he rose and walked out of the barn.

"You must be feeling better, to be offering yourself so freely to that merchant," Meji snapped as soon as Jeth was out of earshot. "All this pretty talk of being kin amuses me. When will he tell you if you are to be his slave, his servant, or his concubine? When you arrive in his land and cannot escape him?"

"I have offered him nothing," I said, "and you should not say such things, or listen in when others are speaking alone."

"Now I am not good enough to hear your conversations with a rich man? Your kinship goes to your head." He folded his arms. "You know you belong here, Deborah, with us. We are your family. Not him."

"Come and sit with me." I patted the empty space beside me. "I have little time, and much to say to you."

"Why should I listen? You have little time. You must go with your new rich friend." He turned his back toward me. "Is that why you would have me play ram to that silly kitchen wench's ewe? So that I would not care when you left with him?"

He was so hurt, but I knew the cause. Meji and I had been together since we were children. In his eyes, it must appear as if I truly were abandoning him.

"Wadina is young, and a little reckless with love, but she will be a good wife to you." Since he would not come to me, I went over to him and held out my hands. "Meji, I have not accepted Jeth's offer, but I think I must. He has been in my dreams for many years now, and we are of the same tribe. That has to mean something. If he truly meant me harm, why would he save me from being beaten to death?"

He turned his back on me. "You know nothing about him. You know only what he has told you. He says he is a merchant, but what if he sells women instead of sheep? Perhaps he saved you because he knows your value on the block. He could cast you in some pit of a brothel in Ephraim to service whoever offers a bit of silver. He could worship filthy gods to whom he sacrifices lambs and babies."

"I have seen only goodness in him." I came around him so that I could see his face. It was wet with tears. "Oh, Meji." I opened my arms. "I will miss you, too."

I was holding his head against my shoulder and rubbing his back when Tarn came to us. "We have separated the finest ewes and rams from the flock for Adon Lappidoth, but he will not leave. I think he will only go with you, Deborah."

Meji smothered a sound and lifted his head to glare at me. "The sun is already high overhead; there are only a few hours of light left. You will need all of them to drive the animals to the riverbank." He touched my face. "Go now."

I kissed his work-scarred hand and pressed it to my cheek before I went out into the sunlight.

Parah and Jeth were waiting there by a wagon filled with supplies. The scribe held a scroll case, which he handed to me as I joined them. "This document ends your enslavement, Deborah. I have made a copy, which as your last owner I will keep. Should you ever need to prove your status, I will witness to it."

I had thought the shock of being freed was over, but again it made me feel dizzy. I took a deep breath to steady myself.

"I thank you for my freedom, Adon Parah." I saw the farmworkers had gathered, and remembered the king's decree. "What will happen to the others? They, too, are mostly Hebrews."

"I expect I will be writing up many more scrolls in the days to come," Parah said, "for I do not own slaves; I employ only free men. Those who are Hebrew may wish to leave Hazor and work on one of my other properties outside King Jabin's territory. I will see to it that they are transported safely."

I remembered seeing Meji working on a farm in the mountains. "You are beyond generous."

"I have reason to be." He tapped the place

on his arm where his sleeve covered the old, terrible scar.

Jeth looked over at the barn. "Your friend was upset."

"It is always difficult to part from friends, and Meji and I grew up together," I explained.

His eyes crinkled with his smile. "You are leaving this place, then?"

"Yes, Adon Lappidoth. I would like to make the journey to Ephraim with you."

I refused to ride in the supply wagon when we left the farm, and instead walked with Jeth and the shepherds to help them drive the herd to the river. My back, though still painful, did not trouble me too much, and it felt good to stretch my legs. Also, I did not want Jeth to think me weak or incapable. I suspected he was acting out of gratitude, but if I could prove that I could be truly useful, then he would never have reason to regret his kindness.

There was a small group of beggars outside the town gate who gathered as our herd approached it. To my astonishment, Jeth stopped the supply wagon to distribute some food and skins of wine and milk from his supplies to the poor folk. I could not look upon their grateful faces, for it was too easy to imagine myself there, huddled among the wretched homeless, thin hands outstretched to every passing stranger, begging for food and kindness.

"The Gods rejoice in the generous, Adon," an elderly, one-legged Canaanite proclaimed as he was given a loaf of bread and a bulging skin of sheep's milk. "For this, I dare say they will see to it that you never know any want in this lifetime."

"I thank you, zaqen, for there is no greater blessing than that," Jeth said with such sincere respect that the old soldier's eyes gleamed with satisfaction and pride.

To reach the river we had to cross through Hazor. Driving the noisy herd through the center of town required some finesse, but the shepherds and their dogs regularly brought animals to auction, and so had much practice passing through Hazor's crowded, narrow streets. I lagged behind the herd, keeping a sharp eye out for tiring lambs or frightened ewes.

Jeth did not lead the herd, but stayed with me. "You will tell me if you grow weary."

I hid a smile. I was accustomed to rising

before dawn and working until well past dusk, no matter how sore or tired I felt. "Yes, Adon."

He made a tsking sound. "You have no master, Deborah. You are a free woman now, and we are kin. Call me Jeth."

"A scroll cannot cause twenty-two years of habit to vanish," I said. "Please forgive me if I forget to use your given name . . . Jeth." It was how I thought of him, and yet it felt audacious to say it out loud.

"Deborah." Soravel, one of the shepherds, dropped into step with us. "We pass by the magistrate's bayit, there." He pointed to a squat building set back from the street. "Our former master watches through the front left window."

It took a few moments for the herd to move ahead, and for us to draw close to the front of the structure. Like Parah's town house, the building served as both the magistrate's home and place of business, but also as a prison for citizens under judgment. I spotted two fists curled around the vertical window slats, and the angry face pressed against them.

"You need not look at him," Jeth said, trying to draw me around and put himself between me and the bayit.

"No." I felt strangely hot and cold as I stopped and stared at the man who had done so much evil in the name of his family. There was only one task left to me. "May I speak to him?"

Jeth nodded but walked with me toward the prison window.

Ybyon's knuckles bulged as he saw me. "Those are my sheep," he called out in a loud, plaintive voice. "These men driving them are my shepherds. I have been robbed by this lying Hebrew. Does no one hear me?"

I went to stand before the window, but had to step aside as my former master spat at me. It was hard not to keep going and leave behind this man who had been the cause of so much of my pain. "I wish to say something to you."

"I do not converse with slaves," he snarled at me before calling out again. "Has Hazor been conquered? Does Jabin fear Barak so that he would allow a Hebrew dog to dictate the fate of a free Canaanite?"

People along the street passed by without giving Ybyon a single look. Judging by the lack of reaction and the faint rasping sound in his voice, it seemed that he had been shouting at them for some time.

In that moment I felt every lash mark on my back as keenly as when they were made, but I tried again. "I wish to say that—"

"Did you not hear me, merchant's whore?" he shouted, at the same time yanking at the unmovable slats. "Get away from me."

It was terrible to look upon the hatred in his eyes, and hear it hurled at me in his words, but I had to do this. Not simply say the words, but also mean them. Even if he did not listen. Even if they meant nothing to him.

"I wish to say that I forgive you for all the wrongs you have done to me." I straightened my shoulders, ignoring the discomfort of my back as I added, "And I forgive you for killing my mother."

"You stupid slut." His jaw tightened, and I heard the sound of teeth grinding together. "I should have cut your scrawny throat while your mother's blood was still fresh on my blade."

I clasped my hands together and bowed my head, as I had so many times in the past. It seemed fitting to do so, not as a slave, but as a free woman he could no longer harm.

"May the One and True God be merciful to you." I reached out and touched his hand, and then I saw what Dasah had always tried to conceal from me. I removed my hand. "I will pray for you . . . Father."

CHAPTER
13

Enraged, Ybyon began shouting again, but I paid no attention to his threats and insults. My soul felt cleansed of the last trace of darkness that his shadow had always cast over my life. I knew I would not think of him again with anything but pity.

Jeth came to my side and peered down at me. "You show him kindness and respect? After all that he has done to you."

Apparently he had not heard the last thing I said to Ybyon. Which was well, as I was still reeling from learning the truth about my parentage.

No wonder Tarn never wished to speak of

my mother, or let me touch him. He had feared I would see the truth about Dasah and Ybyon—but why? Had he known my mother's shame? Had she felt guilt? Ybyon had been her master; she would have had no choice but to surrender herself to him. I could not imagine the master asking politely if she would relieve his needs. Was that why Tarn had not told me?

"Deborah?"

Jeth's concerned voice rid me of my unwelcome thoughts. "'Revile not he in whose steps you may someday walk,'" I said, quoting Tarn's favorite proverb. "I know the path he will follow now only too well." I saw the town gate ahead and heard the shepherds whistling to their dogs. "We are almost there." I forced myself to smile up at him. "I have never seen a boat, much less sailed on one."

"The first journey I made by water was a trading trip with my father on the sea, from Dor to Sidon," Jeth said. "The ship rocked so that I spent the first three days deathly ill, losing my meals over the side and wishing I was dead. Happily, river travel does not have quite the same effect."

"I am glad to hear it." So was my belly. I

did not have so many meals that I could afford to lose any.

I knew from Chemesh's tales of the Sea People that water vessels came in all shapes and sizes, and could be as small as a wagon or as large as a barn. But when we reached the docks outside town, the sight of those waiting for Jeth and his herd astonished me.

Three long, flat boats made of wood floated at the end of sturdy ropes tied to a walkway that began on land and ended in the water. Images of strange animals and people had been painted on the sides, and at each end was an upright, carved wooden statue of a large man's body with a bulging, rather terrifying animal's head. The top of the boats were fashioned of smooth planks, the edges railed with tight bundles of reeds. Each boat was so large that the contents of the farm's stable might have fit comfortably on each one.

"Do they belong to you?" I asked Jeth, awed by the size and beauty of the strangely elegant vessels.

"No, I hired them for the journey before coming to Hazor. I make river trips only every three or four years." He lifted a hand to wave to one of the men standing on the nearest boat. "These are owned by Egyptians who hire their barges out to traders and travelers all along the river. As long as their price is met, they will transport anything." He walked forward toward the man from the boat, who had leapt nimbly onto the half-floating walkway and was coming to greet him.

I looked back over my shoulder at Hazor. It seemed small now, not at all so grand and intimidating as it had the night I met Jeth in town. For a moment I thought of the farm beyond the town, and Meji and the friends I had left behind there. *May Jehovah and Parah watch over you and keep you safe.*

Traveling by river from Hazor to Ephraim took many days. The long, flat boats made slow progress, owing to the needs of the herd Jeth had purchased. Although the sheep and goats numbered fewer than one hundred, and could be watered and fed baled grass and grain from troughs set on the straw-covered flat deck, the animals still needed some exercise and a chance to forage. Thus we stopped at likely spots along the riverbank and drove them across wide ramps so that they could spend some hours grazing.

At first Jeth had wanted to mask the aggressive young rams by strapping a piece of leather over their faces, which he said would keep them from butting each other. It was a foreign method and intrigued me, for rams were natural fighters, but I guessed it was more for the pen and might hinder open grazing. I showed him our way of using a clogging strap, made from a piece of wood and a leather thong.

"It does not interfere with his movement, or hurt him," I said as I strapped the wood to the ram's foreleg. "But he feels the weight of it, and will not charge another ram as long as he wears the strap."

When we stopped to graze the herd, the bargemen, all dusky-skinned Egyptians who kept their heads shaved and wore little more than abbreviated ezor, would take advantage of that time to clean the decks. First they used odd-looking, long-handled brooms to sweep the soiled straw off the side of the deck, and then they tossed bucket after bucket of water across the planks to rinse the wood clean. After the sun dried the wood, they spread fresh straw and scrubbed out the water and feed troughs.

I was fascinated by the bargemen. They spoke little of our language, so we communicated largely by gestures. With each other they chattered openly in their native tongue, which sounded like exotic music to my ears.

Although the bargemen spent most of their lives on the water, with no real home but the decks of their boats, they loved and revered animals. Jeth's goats and sheep were treated with respect and affection, as if they were beloved children instead of herd animals. The men who worked on the barge also appreciated the pans of milk we shared with them each evening, something I guessed was a treat they did not often enjoy. In return, they gave us some of the fish they caught each day, served crisply fried on the flat, seeded lehem they baked on wide stones heated by the boat's braziers.

At first I was reluctant to taste the fish— Ybyon had denied us meat of any kind—but Jeth insisted I have a portion, and he skillfully removed the thin bones for me. "You will like it."

I put a small morsel in my mouth and chewed. The bargemen used strange spices on their food, but they enhanced the savory taste, and I smiled. "It is wonderful."

"It is not something you should grow accustomed to," Jeth warned.

"Oh no, I would never . . ." I saw the twinkle in his eye. "Why not?"

"We must get our fish from the river Kishon, which is many miles from my home," he told me. "I do not wish you to acquire a taste for something I cannot provide. If you do, before we reach Ephraim I may lose you to a bargeman who is clever with a fishing line."

I chuckled and assured him I did not like the fish *that* much.

Nighttime on the river was peaceful and filled with the sounds of crickets and the few frogs that had not retreated into their burrows for the winter. The bargemen poled their way to the bank, then tossed over the heavy sacks of stone tied to the four corners of the boat to moor it there until morning, for in the dark they could not navigate.

Jeth had great plans for his new animals. He told me of them one evening after we had finished milking the herd, and had settled them down on the deck for the night.

"I have needed more rams to breed my

own ewes. If I can keep the new ones healthy, our flock should increase by three hundred come spring." He checked the eyes of one lamb curled up by its mother and gently used a soft cloth to remove some debris from the eyelid. "My hope is to employ all the shearers on the mountain next year."

"Do you sell much wool and goat hair from your herds?" I asked, curious about how he managed his flocks' resources.

"All that I can spare," he said. "My household is large, however, and uses about half what the flocks produce for our needs. I must sell weaned lambs every year to make up the difference."

No wonder he was making trips to buy new animals. I thought for a moment. "What of your dairy?"

He took a small knife from his belt to cut away a knot of burrs in the wool of one ewe's flank. "My grazing land causes the sheep to give sweet milk, so our cheese and butter are highly prized, but that, too, is mostly used by the household."

"You might invest in more goats," I suggested as I checked the clogging strap on one of the older rams. "They do not require as much sweet forage or attention as sheep, and yet they give twice the milk." I hesitated. "Hebrews do like goat's milk?"

He nodded. "Very much."

I went around to extinguish the torches we had lit to encourage the flock to climb the ramps onto the boat, and to check dividers, made of bundles of reed so piled as to keep the herd from following their instincts and gathering in one corner of the deck, which Jeth said would unbalance the boat.

The weather was growing colder by the day, and I shivered as a damp, chilly breeze came up from the east. I had always thought it a shame that people did not grow warm, woolly coats, and were dependent on sheep to let us share theirs. The sudden thought of Seres covered in gray fleece with curling horns at both temples made me giggle.

A hand touched my back. "What makes you laugh?"

"I was imagining Seres, the kitchen steward, as he might look as a ram." I put my forearms against the deck rail and watched the moonlight sparkling on the waves. "It is so beautiful here on the river. I can understand why the bargemen would spend their lives traveling it."

"I should never have let you taste that

fish," Jeth said in a mock-grave tone. "I knew it would spoil you for Ephraim."

"What is Ephraim like?" I knew only the farm, and a little of Hazor.

"Where we live in the mountains is beautiful in spring and summer. Colder and less green during the fall and winter," he admitted. "We would do better if we could move our farms into the valleys, but since the time of Ehud, the Canaanites have gradually taken them from us, as we have little defense against their chariots and pikemen."

"Who is Ehud?"

He gave me a startled look, and then relaxed. "Forgive me. The story of my ancestor is the first one told to every child in the tribe, but of course you would not know. Ehud was a great man; a judge of Israel."

"A judge." I pondered that. "Are your judges like the magistrates in Hazor?"

"More so to us. Our judges are chosen from the wisest men of the tribe, and they interpret God's law. They settle our disputes and guide us through terrible times," Jeth said. "In Ehud's day, our people had allowed themselves to become corrupted by the Moabites, and much of Israel had fallen into sinful ways. Losing their faith with Jehovah allowed Eglon, the king of Moab, to drive them out of the fertile valleys and into the mountains."

I frowned. Such a thing would not happen in Hazor, for like many Canaanite kings, Jabin was said to be meticulous about keeping his army well-armed and at constant readiness. "Could they not fight back?"

"The Moabites viewed us as invaders, and they were very determined to take the land from us," Jeth admitted, "and so gathered mercenaries from among the Rephaim to help them. Even when our people had fled the valleys, Eglon inflicted many more cruelties upon them for a span of eighteen years. Then came Ehud, son of Gesa, who rose up to defy the Moabite tyranny. He told the tribe that Jehovah had spoken to him, and would permit no more abuse of Israel at the hands of Eglon."

"What happened next?" I asked, shivering from the cold but caught up in the suspense of the tale.

"With only the power of his vision, Ehud raised an army of ten thousand men from the tribes and trained them in the ways of battle." Jeth paused to remove his outer kesut and drape it over my shoulders. "When they were ready, he told them that he would strike the first blow against Moab alone."

I frowned as I absently drew his cloak around me. "If that were so, then why did he make an army?"

"I think he knew he would need them later." Jeth grinned. "Ehud went with a caravan carrying tribute to King Eglon—our tribes had to pay all manner of unreasonable tribute to Moab to keep them from slaughtering our settlers—and directed the bearers to lay out the finest Israel had sent before the king. Then he sent the bearers from the room and told the king that if he would also send away his lackeys and guards, he would give him the word of God. Eglon, being a greedy man, was intrigued, and so dismissed his court so he could be alone with Ehud."

"That was silly," I commented. "The king in Hazor would not have done that. He would have had Ehud imprisoned and had the word of God beaten from him."

"It is good that Ehud did not have to face Jabin, then," Jeth said wryly. "As soon as they were alone, Ehud locked all the doors and then told Eglon he would have to rise from his throne to receive the word of God."

The side of his mouth curled. "We imagine that this took a few minutes, for the king was said to be an obese man, but at last Eglon got to his feet and demanded the word."

I leaned closer. "So? What did Ehud tell him?"

"He delivered the word of God," Jeth said. "He drew his sword from his right hip and thrust it into the king's belly, slaying him on the spot. Then he made his escape, leaving the king to be found dead, alone, still locked in his throne room."

I gaped. "Never say he did." What sort of man had the audacity to slay a king in his own palace? I thought about it for a moment. "Wait, if Ehud locked himself in the room, and the king was found dead in the locked room, then how could he have escaped?"

"The stories about him say Jehovah whisked him from the court and took him back to the mountains," Jeth said, "but my father was kin to Ehud's family, and said it was no miraculous thing. After Ehud slew Eglon, he used a rope to scale the wall and climbed through an open skylight in the roof." He spread his hands. "Thus Ehud became legend."

"But what happened when the Moabites

discovered their king slain?" I demanded. "Surely they did not surrender to Israel just like that?"

"No, they marshaled their forces, but the terrifying manner in which Eglon had been slain frightened them, and it was said that they went into battle feeling cursed and defeated by Jehovah." Jeth caught a strand of my hair blowing across my eyes and tucked it back into the cable of my braid. "The Moabites were met in the mountains and the valleys by Ehud and his army, who were waiting for them, and there soundly defeated. For eighty years after, our tribes dwelled in peace, until the Canaanite kings began to invade the land of Moab, and the harassment and persecution began all over again. Today it is almost as bad for us as it was for the tribes before Ehud rose up."

Tarn had told me some other tales of how Hebrews were made to fight over and over for their right to Israel. It did not seem fair that so many wished to steal the land God had promised them.

"You have no one now like Ehud to drive the Canaanites away?" I asked.

Jeth shook his head. "Our judges are still the wisest men of the tribes, but none have received direction from Jehovah on how to engage this new enemy. It was said that a mighty judge would come in the last of the line of Ehud, but it is said that his last descendent died many years ago with no children."

Thanks to Jeth's warm, thick cloak, I did not feel the cold of the wind, but something just as chilling passed through me. "Not all old stories are true," I said, feeling very uneasy.

"No, but I am selfish enough to wish that this one were." Jeth looked out over the water toward the south, and his tone became grim. "I love the land of my father, and my tribe, but each year I see more and more of it claimed by greedy invaders who murder and drive off Hebrew settlers. I fear that they will stop at nothing to take it from us. If we do not soon answer their challenge, then surely this time we will be the ones who are driven out."

CHAPTER
14

Our journey did not end when the bargemen docked a few days later in the southern land belonging to the tribe of Benjamin, for we still had to drive the sheep a short distance down a road that passed through two mountains. Beyond them stood a third, Mount Palma, where Jeth told me his farm and village lay.

"It is only a few hours' walk from the riverbank," he promised me. "I can send a runner to fetch a wagon, if you are weary and would rather ride."

"I would rather walk, please," I said, looking out over the green and fertile plains spreading out before the majestic mountain ranges. "I fear my legs are weary of doing nothing."

I had enjoyed the novelty of traveling by river, but I was glad to step off the boat onto the pier. This night, Jeth promised me, we would sleep under a roof, not in slings beneath a hide canopy over the deck, and our beds would not sway in time to the currents of the river.

The sheep and goats were happy to return to the land, as well. Although they were a little thin from the journey—even the best feed could not keep them as fat as daily grazing and foraging—their eyes were bright and alert and their movements energetic. The sheep's fat tails bobbled as they walked, a sign of contentment, and all the lambs were now sturdy enough to keep up with the herd. Still, I kept to my place at the back and watched for predators in this new land.

Jeth spent some time directing the shepherds at the front of the herd before dropping back to walk with me.

"You did not eat much of the morning meal," he mentioned. "Are you feeling well?"

"I was too excited to eat much." I looked up at the endless stretch of mountains that seemed so much broader and higher than those in Hazor, and I sighed. "It is lovely here. So wild and untamed, the way it is said the world was when our Heavenly Father created it."

"There are many beauties that await your discovery," he promised. "So, when we reach the farm, what would you most like to have?"

I pretended to think hard.

"Never say fish," he teased. The bargemen had been especially lucky in the catch over the last several days, and shared it with us, so most of what we had been eating was fish of one kind or another.

"If I did, I would have stayed on the boat." Something in the distance caught my attention, and I pointed to it. "Jeth, what is that? A cloud of dust?"

He tensed and squinted against the sun, and then relaxed. "No, it is only an escort." At my blank look, he added, "Our tribe sends armed men daily to protect traders and merchants who come by river. It is the only way to keep the Canaanite raiders from attacking them."

The escort turned out to be a dozen warriors who trotted to us at such a quick pace that they stirred up the dust on the road. As they reached the herd, they fell into two lines on either side and marched with us. Their leader, an older man in a leather helmet and armor, came to speak with Jeth.

"Glad I am to see you, Adon Lappidoth." He slapped his hand to his breast in some manner of salute. "With all the activity to the north of us, your kinsmen have been worried you might not return with ease from your journey. Have you word for us on what is happening there?"

"I was in Hazor when King Jabin issued the Hebrew deportation decree. He is stirring up the citizens there to feel most hostile toward our people." Jeth saw the direction of the soldier's gaze and gestured to me. "This is Deborah, a kinswoman of mine from the north. Deborah, this is Captain Avash, commander of the tribal militia and one of the guardians of our tribe."

"Captain." I bowed my head as Jeth had taught me in Hebrew fashion.

"Lady." He returned the gesture. "Excuse my hurriedness, but there is much I must relay to Adon Lappidoth about our situation here."

Jeth's gaze went to the mountains, and a line appeared between his smooth eyebrows. "Have things grown so much worse?"

"Sisera has invaded and occupied Haroshet, and now has command of the only pass from Jezreel into the north of Haifa," Avash stated flatly, as if this were a terrible thing. "His armies have blockaded the roads from Galilee to the Jordan Valley and the Great Sea, which has cut off most of the north trade."

"He thinks to choke us out," Jeth muttered. "What is being done? Have forces been rallied?"

"Not as of yet, Adon. The elders are conferring with our judges, and the tribes have all promised to send as many men as can be spared from protecting the settlements." The worry lines around Avash's eyes and mouth deepened. "Unfortunately there is much squabbling about who will lead them, and when, and where."

Jeth sighed. "Surely the tribal leaders can set aside their differences for this occasion and elect one general for our defense?"

"It is not so simple, I fear. To lead the army into the fray when the signs say it will be decided on the first battlefield requires cold nerve. Then there is the matter of matching the enemy's weapons. Our smiths are forging swords and spears day and night, and the men train, but to hope to prevail against Canaanite chariots and pikes . . ." The older man shook his head. "It will take a remarkable warrior to face down the enemy, and few of our younger leaders have any battle experience. The older fear they will be blamed for losing a war that cannot be won."

I remembered Jeth's story about Ehud, and how the Hebrew tribes had lived in peace for the last eighty years. As he had predicted, it seemed that time was coming to an end.

"What of the temple priests?" Jeth was asking the captain. "Have they not been able to divine Jehovah's will?"

"All the word from the high holy places is the same: There will be two leaders who will come soon." Avash did not sound convinced. "One will be a judge, and the other general. They will lead us to victory."

"When?" Jeth demanded, sounding frustrated now.

Avash sighed. "I cannot say, but I hope it is soon. With the north trade routes under Jabin's control, and Sisera controlling the gentile tribes at Haroshet, our days in this land may be counted on a single breath."

*   *   *

Captain Avash rejoined his men and remained with them as we crossed through the pass. Jeth did not speak to me of what they had discussed, and since I knew nothing of the names and places they had mentioned, I did not ask any questions. Still, our silence was a companionable one, and it lasted until we reached the base of the mountain Jeth called home.

The first sign of settlement I saw was a little village, sitting halfway up the base slope on a wide shelf of earth.

"That is Palma," Jeth said, pointing to the tight circular cluster of dwellings and pens.

Palma was perhaps only the width and breadth of three streets in Hazor, so at first it appeared quite small to my eyes. As we drove the herd up the gently sloping road to the village, I saw the houses and business built there were nestled very close together, and numbered at least sixty or seventy.

Beyond the village were other plateaus that had been cultivated into farm lands and fenced pastures. On these wider, open areas I saw rough-hewn fences, and behind them many flocks of sheep, goats, and cattle.

From the look of the mountain, many such wide, flat shelves of earth climbed like steps along the mid-region, but they did not appear naturally formed. The settlers here must have spent many months toiling to level great stretches for more practical use.

"I wish I could have shown you our homeland for the first time during the spring," Jeth said to me as he watched me taking in the view ahead. "Just after the last of the heavy rains, the sun warms the mountain back to life, and the first wheat we plant sprouts. It covers the hills and pastures like a pale green mist. There are entire fields of wildflowers, too, of all the colors of the rainbow. So many that my mother complains she has never enough pots and urns to put them in for the house."

I knew from our many conversations during the river journey that Jeth's father had died of coughing sickness five winters past, and that as his eldest son, Jeth had inherited the position of head of the family. His younger brothers had chosen to go into trade in Rameh, and his only sister had died shortly after birth, so just his mother and her maids lived in his home with him at the farm.

The thought of now meeting his mother, however, worried me.

"You are sure I will not cause any trouble

arriving like this, with no warning?" Ybyon's wife had made a great fuss of the few visitors who came to stay at the farm, and caused Seres and the kitchen slaves extra work for days preparing grand meals.

"My mother often berates me for not inviting more guests to the farm," he said. "She will be delighted to meet you."

I did not know how protective free Hebrew women were of their sons, but I suspected that Jeth's mother would wish to know who I was, and why I had come here from Hazor. That I might be a distant kinswoman did not seem enough reason, and I might alarm her with the tale of Ybyon's treachery.

I have not even told Jeth that Ybyon was my father, I thought, feeling my insides curdling. What if his mother asked about my family? I could not lie. *Perhaps I will hold my tongue and let him explain everything.*

I thought one of the smaller farms along the village road might belong to my benefactor, but he directed the shepherds to drive the herd past them and take a side path that cut across one of the large open pastures. At the other side were more fenced paddocks, and a low, wide farm house.

"You should keep the new animals separated from those here," I said to Jeth. "Some
may have grown sick from the journey, but
you may not be able to tell for several days."

"All will be penned away from my flocks
until we know they are healthy," he agreed.

As we drew closer, I saw that the farmhouse was enormous: a dwelling large
enough to support four or five extended
families—perhaps twice or even three times
as large as my former master's main house,
which by Canaanite standards had been
considered quite grand.

"You do not like it?" Jeth asked me.

I dragged my gaze from the smoothly
plastered golden brick walls and the roof of
strangely tied bundles of thatch. "It seems
like the palace of a king."

"My father was a large man like me," he
explained, taking my arm in his. "He liked
having room. He also brought his family here
to live until they could clear good pastureland and build dwellings of their own."

Before the last sheep had passed into the
paddock gate, a trio of figures came walking
from the farmhouse. The first was a white-
haired woman in elegantly plain robes dyed

a lovely shade of light blue, followed by two younger, dark-haired women dressed in the practical garments of maidservants.

"Is this my firstborn come back from the north land, Captain Avash?" the older woman asked the commander of our escort. She herself had a commanding voice and stern eyes, and a large, soft brown birthmark at the right corner of her lips. "Or have you captured some thieving raider trying to steal the best from our flocks?"

Avash hid a smile by bowing deeply. "I will let you decide that, Lady Urlai."

"Mother." Jeth laughed and went to her, and he swept her up in his arms as if she were no more than a child. "How glad I am to see you."

"Glad you are, when you spend months away from your family, and worry me so that I cannot rest more than an hour or enjoy more than a bite or two of any meal? I should have one of the girls fetch a switch, that I may thrash you proper." The Lady Urlai kissed her son soundly and hugged him close.

Jeth laughed. "You see? You are glad I am home."

"No, now that I think about it, I believe *I*

shall travel to the north country, and you may stay here and spend *your* nights pacing the floor." She looked past her son and saw me for the first time, and her smile disappeared. "Jeth, who is this with you?"

I stepped forward with great hesitancy, for I saw no delight in the lady's eyes. I was not sure of how to introduce myself, or even if it were proper that I should, so I made a polite bow and looked to Jeth.

He held out his hand, and took mine to lead me forward. "Mother, this is Deborah of Hazor. Her mother was our kinswoman, a daughter of the tribe of Benjamin."

"Indeed," Urlai said in a low voice as she inspected me from head to foot. "I did not know we had kin in the north land."

"Very distant kin, lady," I said, and grimaced. My throat was so tight, it was making my voice squeak.

"Distance is nothing among the tribe." Urlai produced a ferocious frown. "I truly should beat my son. Why has he not been feeding you properly? You are as thin as a chafe stick."

"I have never eaten better in my life than during this journey to Ephraim, lady," I assured her. "I am very glad to meet you at last. Jeth has told me so much about you and your home."

"Has he." Urlai stepped closer, peering into my eyes. When I went still, she shook her head. "Do not be afraid, child. I am an old woman, but my memory has yet to fail me, and glad I am of it." She kissed both my cheeks. "You are welcome here, Deborah of Hazor. Forgive me my strangeness, but it is not often that I can return to my girlhood. I never thought to look into such wondrous eyes again."

"Mother?" Jeth sounded a little worried now.

"You are tired and thirsty and hungry," Urlai said, sounding practical. She put an arm around my shoulders. "Come inside now, and let me show you a proper meal."

I glanced back at Jeth, who looked as confused as I felt. "You are certain that you do not mind me visiting?"

Urlai looked at me, astounded. "Visiting? Oh, child, do you not know?" She smiled, making the round brown mark by her mouth disappear into her dimpled cheek, and kissed my cheek again. "You are among your people. You are home at last."

*   *   *

The next hours passed in a blur of excellent food served in the large and airy room at the center of the farmhouse, where Urlai dismissed her maidservants and served us herself.

"You must tell me everything that happened on your journey," the lady said as she ladled a rich mutton broth into bowls for us. "Why did you take so long? I expected you home when the moon was full, a week past. Were there any difficulties with the Canaanites?"

Jeth answered her questions in a very vague way, speaking mostly about the sheep and goats he had obtained in Hazor, but he did not recount the story of Ybyon's treachery or how I had intervened.

I concentrated on eating my soup without spilling it all over the fine table his mother had set for us.

During the conversation with his mother, the only thing Jeth mentioned about Hazor other than the crowded streets and the fine work Parah had done for him was the king's decree to deport all resident and visiting Hebrews.

"You know that Jabin has caused much grief among the tribes throughout the land," Urlai told her son after we had finished eating. "Captain Avash likely told you the latest news. The tribal leaders are spreading the word about the blocked roads and towns now hostile toward us, so that those who travel can avoid them."

"Has there been any word from the tabernacle on what we are to do?" Jeth asked.

"None. But the signs that have so troubled our priests are about to be made clear, I believe." Urlai turned her gaze on me. "You must be exhausted with only the company of men, my dear. I will show you to the women's quarters, where you can bathe and rest." She gave Jeth a stern look. "You may go and greet your shepherds, who have long been suffering your absence and have plagued me with many complaints about the market price of grain and wool and such ridiculous matters."

"Yes, Mother. Deborah, I will see you in the morning." After giving me a sympathetic smile, Jeth left us.

Urlai rose and gestured to me. "Come, Deborah."

"I do not have to sleep in the house," I said as I followed her out of the room and down a long hallway. "Any place will do, really."

"Where has my son made you sleep, that you would say such a thing?" Urlai demanded.

I should have said nothing, but I felt awkward being alone with her now. "It is just that I . . . I do not wish to be a burden."

"We have much to discuss," she said, and put her arm around me again. "And tomorrow we will. Tonight, you shall be made comfortable and rest—inside this house, if you please."

I desperately wanted to escape to the nearest barn or shed, and hide in the straw, but I made myself walk meekly with Urlai into the room at the end of the hall.

The women's quarters were occupied by several maidservants, two exotic-looking birds in beautiful cages made of painted twigs, and simple but comfortable-looking sleeping and bathing areas. At the lady's insistence, I undressed behind a screen and washed myself thoroughly in the large tub of warm water placed there by her maids.

"Here you are—I believe this will fit you." Urlai hung a length of linen for drying and a clean, soft robe over the top of the screen. "How old are you, Deborah?"

"I am two and twenty years, I think," I said as I dried off my limbs and slipped into the robe.

"You do not know?"

Should I tell her I was slave-born? "My mother died when I was very small, and those who cared for me did not often make mention of it."

Urlai made a *hmmmm*ing sound. "What of your father? Did he not know the day of your birth?"

"I never knew him when I was growing up." I thought desperately of how I might change the subject. "Is there some work I can do here, Lady Urlai? I can clean and mend a little, but mostly I know how to care for sheep, and other animals."

Jeth's mother was silent for a long time, until she finally said, "You need not worry about that now, child. Come, let me show you where you are to sleep."

I was more weary than I realized, for hardly a few moments after Urlai covered me with a light blanket did my eyes close and my thoughts dissolve into the blessed blankness of sleep.

For a long time I rested in the safe haven of darkness, but then I was taken into a dream. I found myself not idling in the garden of Jehovah, but standing alone in the middle of a quiet golden valley. I could see snow on the peaks of the mountains to the west and east, but there was nothing else save grass and the land and me, and I did not know the place.

I spotted two paths, each leading in different directions, and moved toward one that was lined on both sides with clusters of red and yellow flowers.

"Hold." A powerful-looking figure in a dark cloak appeared before me, and held up a sword as if to strike me. "Do you choose the path of the heart, or the path of faith?"

"I choose the path with the flowers." I did not recognize the voice, but I kept my eyes on the sword. "Who are you?"

Lightning divided the sky and struck the ground between us with a thin, jagged blade of white light.

"I am the Summoned," the sword-bearer said, and pulled back the hood of the cloak. The man's face beneath it was harsh and uncompromising. "You hold my fate in your hands."

"I will give it back," I promised. "Only tell me how."

A thin smile appeared on his grim visage. "That is for you to decide, Truth-seer." He turned and pointed to the other path that I had not wished to take, which was rocky and not at all appealing. "If you move in that direction."

I looked up at the sky. "Heavenly Father, I am a simple woman. I know sheep, not warriors and paths and the meaning of dream signs. Please make me understand this."

The man seized my wrist. "We two are one in destiny. We were brought into being to deliver this nation. I cannot be without you. I cannot see without your eyes."

Beyond him I saw Jeth waiting on the path of flowers. He looked miserable, and I knew that if I did not go to him, he would remain so—as would I. "Am I not to know any happiness, then?"

"Your joy is in knowing the will of God," the man told me. "As my life and honor is knowing yours."

"Who are you?" I asked again.

"I am the one you will summon. The lightning from heaven, the pride of Kedesh. Take the path of faith and call me from Naphtali, and I will come. Walk the righteous way, and I will bring ten thousand to follow in your footsteps." The man released me and stepped back, fading from sight as he did so. "Only remember pride, Truth-seer. Remember pride."

CHAPTER
15

A maidservant with a shy smile was waiting with a cup of warm herb tea when I awoke the next morning.

"My lady Urlai wishes you not to rise until you wish to," she told me. "I am happy to fetch you whatever you wish for your morning meal."

I glanced over at the long narrow window and saw bright sunlight. "What hour is it?"

"Almost midday," said the girl.

I pushed back the woven blanket tangled around me and stood. Steady ground felt odd to my legs, so accustomed were they to the rocking of the riverboats. I felt guilty for my laziness. "I should not have slept so long."

"Oh, no, mistress, you need not rise at all. Our lady wishes you to rest as much as you like." The maidservant pressed the cup of tea into my hands. "Let me bring you bread and fruit—or do you wish something else to break your fast?"

I was making the poor girl as nervous as she was me. "What is your name?"

"Eleen, Mistress."

"Eleen, my name is Deborah, not mistress. And I have never slept so late in my life." I took a quick sip of the tea and put the cup back into her hands. "Where is the privy here?"

Eleen showed me to another, smaller chamber that, like the indoor privy at my former master's home, had been arranged to provide for a woman's needs. After I had seen to my own and washed, I came out and asked Eleen to take me to Urlai.

"Our lady rises early each day, for she says she cannot bear to miss the rising of the sun over the mountains," the maidservant said as she escorted me through two passages and into another part of the long farmhouse. "On fair days she has a table brought out into her gardens where we all break fast together."

I had never heard of the lady of a household doing such a thing, but obviously Hebrew ways were different. Still, that was no excuse for my own idleness. I had to earn my keep, and the sooner I learned how I might do that, the happier I would be.

"Is there much work to be done around the house?" I asked Eleen. When she gave me an odd look, I added, "I prefer not to be idle."

"I am the same," she admitted cheerfully. "Once, I had twisted my ankle, and the lady made me stay abed. I thought I might go mad from boredom."

The place Eleen brought me to appeared to be like the weaver's lean-to on the farm. This room, however, was warm and cozy, thanks to a number of large braziers, and held several maidservants who were in the process of carding and rolling freshly washed fleeces for spinning.

Jeth's mother was in the center of things, picking over fleeces and examining them in the light from one of the windows for color and thickness.

"This gray will do well for the heavy kesut cloth," she was saying to one of her girls. "After it is spun, we will soak it in warm water and have the weaver put it on the loom damp. The cloth will be fuller and thicker that way." She looked up and saw me. "Deborah, you are awake."

"At last. I did not mean to sleep so much." I turned and thanked Eleen before going to Jeth's mother. "May I help with the work here?"

Urlai hesitated before she answered with, "I would rather you come with me into the garden. The first of the frost rains came two day past, and I must gather what roots and herbs are left before the next drowns them." She handed the gray fleece to her maid before showing me through a door to the outside.

Tall, broad-leafed winter fig trees hemmed a tilled and tidy patch of garden ground that had been stripped of most of its plants.

"We grow very fine melons in the summer, as well as salad greens, onions, and cucumber," Urlai said as she took a small digging stick from a basket outside the door. To me she handed the empty basket. "Many kinds of beans and lentils and herbs come in early fall, and then we gather the figs and dates, and the root vegetables."

She crouched down by a straggling cluster of green and dug up a gnarled root, the like of which I had never seen.

"What is that?" I asked her.

"These Jeth brought me from a trader to the east he met at market in Rameh. I know not the name they are called, but the root is what is eaten, and I confess that we have grown very fond of its taste. It can be ground as a spice, or chopped and cooked with honey and dates to make a sweet spread for cakes."

I smelled the root, which had a sharp but pleasing scent. "It must taste better than it looks," I mentioned as I regarded its ugly, knobbly exterior.

"Appearances are not always a sign of what is within," Urlai agreed. "Like you, Deborah. From the roughness of your hands and the streaks of sun in your hair, I would guess you have spent much time laboring outside. You are eager to do work here, too, like one of the servants."

I placed the root in the basket and took the next she had dug from her. "I was born a slave in Hazor," I said quietly. "Your son was kind to me, and saw to it that I was freed. He brought me here to meet my kin."

"That explains much," Urlai said as she dusted the soil from her hands, "but not how a daughter of Benjamin could be born in the north country, so far from her tribe."

"I cannot say, lady, for my mother died before she could tell me how she came to be in Hazor." I remembered something Tarn had told me. "She was not born there—I know that. She was brought up from the south. Perhaps her people are somewhere close to here."

Urlai finished digging the last of the roots and placed them in the basket. "I have my own ideas about that, my dear, but that will keep until this evening, when my son returns from the barns." She looked into my eyes, and her expression softened. "It is not easy coming to a new place, is it? And then to be made to confess to a stranger that your life was not as it should have been."

"My life is as it is." I looked down at the pile of roots in the basket. "I am not ashamed of the work I did, or of the people who cared for me." I thought of Ybyon. "There is just so much . . . unhappiness in my past."

"Let us do what we can to keep it there," Jeth's mother said, and touched my arm with a gentle hand. "Now, I have this stubborn nut tree over here that refuses to ripen when it should. Shall we see if it is finally ready to make a contribution to our household?"

I worked in the garden gathering roots and herbs and nuts with Urlai until she declared she was famished and took me to the kitchen to see to a meal. As in the garden, we worked together there, and she showed me the Hebrew way of preparing several different dishes.

"I always have a pot of soup kept warm over the cooking pit during the winter months," she mentioned as we pitted some dates for a sweet lehem she wished to bake for the evening meal. "Nothing warms the belly like a good, thick broth on a cold day."

After we sat at the little table in the kitchen with the maidservants and ate a light meal, Urlai took me back to the workroom, where we sorted and picked over fleeces and carded the wool. The tasks were so simple and easily done that I began to feel guilty again.

"I am very good with animals," I told her as we gathered up the rolls of carded wool that would be bundled and taken to the village weaver. "If you need another hand in the barns, I would be glad to go."

"You have not spent much time on the inside of a house, have you?" she asked.

I glanced around me. "The walls do make me a little uneasy."

"Then we shall take a walk outside, while the weather is still bright," she declared. "For when the heavy rains come, little more than these walls will you be seeing."

I had been on Jeth's farm only a day, so there was much I had not seen. Urlai pointed out the pastures and the different barns beyond the house, and told me of the purposes they served.

"There are some families in the village who are too poor to afford to hire a shearer in the spring, so we have them bring their sheep and goats here," Urlai said of the largest barn where the annual shearing was done. "Once the last fleece has been sent to the washing shed, we have a feast in the center of the village." She stopped and frowned.

I followed her gaze and saw two young boys who were rolling together in the grass a short distance from us. For a moment I thought they were at play, until I saw one strike the other with his fist.

"Hetho, Poal," Urlai called out, causing the pair to cease their tussle. "You boys come here to me."

The two jumped to their feet and hurried over to Jeth's mother. As they ran, Urlai said to me, "These are two of my housekeeper's children. They are permitted to come and help their father herd the goats in from pasture, but usually I do not come upon them pummeling each other."

"Lady Urlai," one of the breathless boys said as they reached us. "Poal stole my crook from the barn and hid it somewhere."

"That is not the truth, lady," Poal insisted. "Hetho has hidden it himself but puts the blame on me."

"Telling a falsehood is a sin," Hetho cried out, pointing at his brother. "You will not say so, but you have wished to take it since Father gave it to me. I know you are jealous, for it is the crook he used as a boy, and as first-born it is to be mine."

"No, it is *you* who are jealous that I am to be sent to apprentice with Adon Remaun," Poal argued. "You wish to cause me trouble so that Father will think me too young and keep me home with our baby sister."

"Hold your tongues, both of you," Urlai commanded, and the boys fell silent but continued to glare at one another. "I had not thought either of you a liar, but it seems that I am wrong." She turned her head and murmured for my ears alone, "If only I could tell which one it is."

I went to the children and rested a hand on their heads. It took only a brief moment to see their truth, and then I crouched down to look into their eyes.

To the younger, I said, "Poal, you were jealous of Hetho being given your father's old crook. You should not envy your brother his place in the family. You are both much beloved by your parents."

Poal hung his head. "But it is not fair, lady. There are two of us, but only one crook."

"You see?" Hetho said, sounding triumphant. "I knew he stole it from me."

I turned to the older boy. "Your brother did *not* steal from you. You were careless and left the crook where you were playing in the hay. You also envy your brother's skillful hands, and do not wish him to go to apprentice to the village carpenter."

Hetho's eyes rounded, and then his chin dropped to his chest. "He is the younger, but everyone will think him more clever than me."

"Envy leads us to sin," I reminded them. "Brothers share a special bond like no other. You must love and defend each other, never attack out of hatred, or you will go the way of Cain and Abel."

Sobered by the reminder of what had happened to the first brothers of man, Poal looked at Hetho. "I am sorry that I punched you when you called me a thief."

His older brother nodded slowly. "And I should not have accused you of stealing when I was careless." He looked up at me. "May we go to the barn to search the hayloft, lady?"

I glanced at Urlai, who nodded, and then I smiled at them. "Go, but be careful on the ladder."

"You have a deft touch with children," Urlai

said. "I would not have been able to ferret the truth out of them so quickly."

"Sometimes," I said, "all it takes is a touch."

The evening meal was much more formal that night, with Urlai sitting at Jeth's right hand, while I was placed at what must have been the guest's place across from Jeth at the cloth-covered table.

After the hot food had been brought from the kitchen, Urlai reached to take my right hand, and Jeth my left, and they also joined their free hands together.

"Is this a Hebrew custom?" I asked.

"A family one," Urlai said. "Will you say the blessing over the meal, Deborah?"

I closed my eyes and tilted my head back. "Heavenly Father, the One and True God of our people, we thank you for this food, the warmth of the fire, and the joy of this home. All our prosperity comes from You. May we show that we are worthy of it, and Your many blessings, each day we live."

Something came over me while my eyes were closed, and I saw eyes like my own, only in the face of a little girl, and another, older child with a small brown birthmark next to her mouth. They were rolling a wheeled toy back and forth between them, on the clay floor of a simple but comfortable room. Two older women, their mothers, sat close by, picking over pans of beans as they watched the children play—

I opened my eyes and released the hands holding mine. Urlai was watching me, as was Jeth, and they both looked concerned.

"Forgive me," I said. "I did not mean to . . . do that."

"Never worry, my dear." Jeth's mother patted my hand. "Now, you must try the fig porridge. It is not so heavy as it looks, and I flavored it with some of the ugly root spice which my son brought me as a gift."

"A gift of which she still boasts over to all her friends," Jeth assured me.

That the two loved each other was only too clear, but the odd manner they had of jesting with each other often startled me. I spent much of my time during the meal listening and trying to fathom their jokes.

When we had finished eating, Urlai sent for cups of spiced tea and asked us both to join her by the fire, as she had a story to tell us.

The Hebrews did not have much furniture,

but they enjoyed reclining on large pillows stuffed with soft wool. I found it another custom that would take some getting used to, for slaves did not have much reason to sit other than to milk sheep or eat.

Once the tea had been served, Urlai dismissed her maidservants and sat back against a pile of pillows, the covers of which were woven in bright stripes of blue and green. "I have a story to tell you, one that has been a mystery to our people since I was a young girl. Most of it my mother told me later, just before she died, so I would know to tell my daughter and keep the tale alive." She sighed. "Unfortunately your sister died when she was a baby, and in not telling, I had almost forgot it."

"Why did you never tell me or my brothers?" Jeth asked.

"Because men do not feel the loss of a child the way women do," Urlai said. "And because the men of my mother's generation almost went to war over this."

I sat up. "Perhaps I should leave you two alone."

"No, Deborah, I think you should hear this." Urlai set aside her tea and stared into the flames. "My grandmother was a skilled midwife, and as was custom in the old times, was the only woman permitted to attend the women of the tribe when they gave birth. She delivered the low and the high, the babies of beggars and of high priests, and held that there was no difference between them. My mother told me that she even delivered Gesala, the daughter and only child of Ehud, the great judge of Israel. She said that the child was born different. She was left-handed, as Ehud was, and had other strangeness about her. My grandmother had never seen the like of her."

"That is Ehud that prophet who slew Eglon?" I asked Jeth.

"The same," he told me.

"Gesala cared for Ehud in his old age, and did not marry until after her father died. She accepted the offer of one of her father's kinsmen from Kedesh, but by then she was an older woman, and so, too, was blessed with but one child. A daughter, born as her mother had been, left-handed, and strange."

"How so strange?" Jeth asked. "Left-handed children are rare, but not so uncommon."

"I will come back to that," his mother said.

"I was born three years before Ehud's granddaughter, and as our parents' farms were close to each other, our families became friends. Like her mother and her grandfather before her, Gesala's daughter was left-handed and in some ways not like other children."

"She must have felt lonely," I said, thinking of how my own differences had made many of the other slaves afraid of me.

"She was, but we played together when we were girls," Urlai said. "I remember her as a small, gentle-natured child, and the only thing I thought strange about her was that she did not like to be touched by anyone but her mother. The tribe had great hopes for Gesala's daughter, as it was predicted that her child would become a great judge of Israel."

"Jeth told me that she died." I gave her a sympathetic look. "How sad."

"That is the time I know least about, for one day she was my playmate, and the next I never saw her again. I remember a morning when Gesala came, weeping and hysterical, to fall into my mother's arms. Then Gesala went away, and other kin took over their farm. Indeed, I would never have known what had happened, had my mother not told me when she grew sick. There had been a raid, you see, while Gesala was visiting friends. Her husband, his brothers, and their daughter had been slain, although they never found the body of the child. It was thought that wild animals had dragged her away. Gesala was the only one of her family to survive."

That must have been worse than knowing her dead. "The poor woman." Impulsively I touched Urlai's hand. "I am sorry about your friend."

"So was I, until yesterday, when you came, child." She gestured to my face. "For you have her eyes."

"I remind you of her?" I was touched. "I hope it does not make you sad."

"In some ways it does, for now I think I know her fate. She was not killed, I believe, but taken by the raiders. It would have been easy to subdue a child, and later sell her to slavers. Given your age, Deborah, Dasah could have been your mother."

"Dasah?" I felt as if my heart might stop. "Dasah was the name of Gesala's daughter?"

Urlai nodded. "Dasah, daughter of Gesala, granddaughter of Ehud." She smiled at Jeth. "A fine choice, I think."

"No." I shook my head and forced an uneasy laugh. "I do not think she and my mother can be the same person. It is only a coincidence of the names."

"But you have her eyes," Jeth's mother insisted. "I have never forgotten them."

"The other slaves on my master's farm said that my mother had been branded a witch, like so." I traced the mark Tarn had described to me across my forehead. "Did your people brand Gesala's daughter?"

"Oh, no, my dear. We would never harm a child so." Urlai turned to Jeth. "You know more about slave traders than I. Are they superstitious enough to brand a little girl they feared?"

"Among the hill people to the west, yes, there are some who fear evil and demons in anything strange. They brand, cut off ears and noses, and even geld boy children born with certain marks or deformities. It is possible they were the ones who took Dasah."

I shook my head. "It cannot be me. I am flattered that you would think me the descendant of such a noble family, but Dasah must be a common name."

"I can tell you that the disappearance of Gesala's child troubled all the women of the tribe," Urlai said. "So much so that no one has named their daughter Dasah for two score years. They feared it might bring bad luck upon the child."

Jeth rubbed his brow. "The hill people are not the only ones with superstitions."

"I never knew my mother," I said, "so I cannot prove or disprove your claim. Though I would rather not claim to be someone I will never be sure I am."

"There is one way to know." Urlai made a circling gesture in front of her nose. "Were you born with a mask of skin here, over your face?"

"Yes, but . . ." I looked helplessly at Jeth. "You told her?"

"I did not know of it myself. I do know the stories of children born thus. They are blessed by Jehovah to be prophets, and judges." He paused and gave me a thoughtful look. "Because they can see what will be, as well as the truth in all other men."

"It is also said that they cannot lie," Urlai put in.

The walls were closing in on me, just as Jeth's mother had predicted. I pushed myself up from the pillows and stood. "May I walk outside?"

"Of course." Urlai looked as if she wished to say more, but then she lapsed into silence.

"I will go with you." Jeth followed me out.

CHAPTER
16

The air outside was cold and damp, herald-
ing the rains of which Urlai had spoken.
Clouds blocked out the stars, and over the
mountains they lit up with lightning from
within. I walked quickly away from the house,
distressed and angry, and wishing to be neither. My benefactor stayed at my side until
we reached the first of the fences protecting
his flocks.

"My mother did not mean to offend you,"
Jeth said.

"It is too much," I said, unsure if I was an-
swering him or reassuring myself. "I know
you to be kind people, and I am grateful for

all you have done. But I cannot be made a replacement for a long-dead child."

"Her body was never found," Jeth pointed out. "Do not be angry at my mother. She sees you, the same age as Dasah's child might be, with the same eyes as her child-hood friend, born different as Gesala and Dasah were. I think it natural for her to make the connections."

"Many children are born with masks of skin. The Canaanites take the skin and keep it in a jar, if you can believe that. They think to destroy it will bring evil upon the baby." I went to the paddock fence and looked out over the slumbering sheep. "There is no need to do this for me. I would be happy to serve you and your mother for the rest of my days. I do not need a new life invented for me. I am not ashamed of what I am."

"If you are Gesala's granddaughter, then why would it be repugnant to you?" He rested a hand on my shoulder. "Ehud was one of our greatest leaders. Your family is gone now, but they were greatly honored."

"You yourself told me of the prophecy," I reminded him. "That the last of Ehud's line would become a judge of Israel." I released a bitter laugh. "Here I am, Jeth. A woman. Worse, a slave woman. What sort of judge will I make, do you think?"

"I cannot say," he admitted. "We have never before had a woman judge."

"You see?" I threw up my hand. "Better you look for another slave woman by the name of Dasah, and see if she has given birth to a son."

He turned me to face him. "I do not understand your anger."

"Do you not?" I nodded toward the house. "You live like a prince here. You have never gone hungry, I think, or lain in the cold, wishing for a blanket. You have never been beaten for an imagined wrong, or been whipped for telling the truth." Tears crowded up in my eyes. "I have no living family. I have never belonged to anyone. Now you would make me something I can never be. Your mother called me a fine choice? Well, I am not. I am no one, nothing. Let me work with the servants, or put me out in the fields with the herds. Give me something that I know, that I understand."

"I should have said something before now, but I did not wish to rush you any more than I have already." He took my hands in his. "Deborah, when my mother spoke of you as a fine choice, she did not mean as Gesala's daughter. Nor did I bring you here to be my servant, or to fulfill an old legend."

Suddenly, deeply ashamed of my outburst, I ducked my head. "I did not expect you to give me work. Of course I will find a position in another household. If you will but recommend me to one of your neighbors—"

"I brought you to my home so that you could meet my mother," Jeth said softly. "I wanted to show you my farm and introduce my family and friends to you. Our tribe is large, so we have many. I want to take you to our temple, so that we may both receive Jehovah's blessing."

"You wish to adopt me?" My mother had explained some Hebrew customs to me, but nothing like this.

"No." He bent and brushed his mouth over mine. "I wish to make you my wife."

It was more of a shock than when Parah had told me I would be freed, but I did not faint this time. I held on to his arms with my hands, convinced the earth would begin rocking under my feet at any moment.

Jeth drew back and looked down at me. "You are still weary from the river journey, and this story of my mother's has unsettled you. Perhaps we should talk about this to-morrow."

"There is nothing to say, except . . . why?"

"Why do I ask you? Well, I know it is proper for a man to go to the woman's family, but they are all gone now." He brushed some hair back from my cheek. "Do you wish me to go to the tribal leaders? They will give consent in place of those who are gone."

"Stop it," I whispered. "If you are not jesting with me, then you must know my answer."

"I do not have your gift for seeing inside people, but I hope the answer is yes." His white teeth flashed. "Is it yes?"

I moved away from him. "You should have said this to me in Hazor. Had I known your intention, I would not have come on this journey with you."

Jeth's easy smile faded. "Why? I know I am asking you to do me a great honor, but you are under no obligation to accept. All you need do is tell me no."

"A great honor, to marry a slave?" I gestured at my shabby clothing. "A woman who has done nothing but take care of sheep, and live like them, all her days? I could see how you might fool yourself into believing me the granddaughter of Gesala, but how could you even think of me as a wife?"

"I have thought of little else since the day we met, when you came running from the storm. Even then, I thought you the most beautiful thing I had seen on my journey." He walked toward me. "And you cannot call yourself a slave anymore. You may be the last of Ehud's line. Even if you are not, you are a free woman now."

"I have been a free woman barely two weeks," I reminded him. He cornered me; to evade him I would have to jump over the fence. Since I did not wish to startle the flock, I stayed where I was and tried to reason with him. "Jeth, you are a wealthy man. Any woman would be honored to be your wife. But you should ask someone who has lived as you have, who knows your people, your ways—"

"Ah, but I want a woman who is strong and practical and brave," he said, running his hand over my long hair. "Strong enough to survive many years of hardship and deprivation. Practical enough to cover her hair with evil-smelling muck and pretend to be a boy to warn a foreigner of danger. Brave enough to take a savage beating and face death rather than betray a stranger to whom she owed nothing. I know of only one woman who is all those things."

I felt desperate and angry. "Are there no unmarried women in this village, that you must make me your choice?"

"There are many women, and many will be disappointed that I did not choose them, but among them I will never find one as courageous and beautiful as you, Deborah." He cupped my cheek. "Say you shall."

"I shall be nothing but trouble for you." Tears welled up in my eyes. "I have a slave brand, no dowry, and a bitter past. I cannot lie. Every time I touch you, I would know if you had lied to me. Is that the woman you wish for a wife?"

"You will make a very honest man out of me." He pulled me into his arms. "Say you will be my wife. Say you will."

I could feel his body, and how desire had changed it. There—there was a way out of this impossible tangle. "If you wish me to service you, I shall do so. You do not have to marry me." I had to be truthful. "I have only seen others do it, and looked away before I saw much, but you could tell me how."

"No, my brave girl." Instead of being amused or offended, he kissed my brow. "Your maiden night is not enough for me. I want you with me forever."

A waking dream rose inside me, for I was touching him, and I could see into his heart in that moment. He did wish me to be his wife. He saw me as so many things: his friend, companion, lover, the mother of his children, the keeper of his home. He hoped that I would grow to love him, too, for without me he would never feel complete again.

Jeth did love me.

I did not think I could be all the things he wanted. All I knew of love was from my mother. But my heart cried out for Jeth, and knowing his feelings made it impossible to deny my own.

"I'm afraid. I do not know what will happen to us if I am . . ." I could not bring myself to claim the mighty lineage of Ehud. Not yet.

"So am I." He held me close. "Say you will anyway, Deborah."

"There is something else you must know." I pulled back a little. "I discovered just before we left Hazor that Ybyon is my father. I saw the truth when I touched him at the magistrate's window. He used my mother for his own pleasure, and then he doubtless threatened to hurt me to make her see for him." I had hoped to dismay him, but he did not seem at all shocked or angered. "Do you still wish me to say I will?"

"I do not care if King Jabin was your father," Jeth said, his voice stern. "I shall have no other." He sighed. "Do you not remember what that old soldier at the beggar's gate said to me? I will know no want or hunger in this lifetime. If I cannot have you, I will go on always wanting."

I could be a slave to the past and live in silent shame because of it, forever. Or I could seize the gift Jehovah offered me: a husband I could cherish, a man I already loved—and possibly the honor of the family I had been denied since birth. "I cannot defy the blessing of an old soldier, I suppose."

He smiled. "They are always right, you know. That is why they live to be so old."

"Very well." I faced him as I did my destiny. "I will be your wife, Jeth, son of Lappidoth."

*   *   *

In proper Hebrew marriages, the betrothal was supposed to last several months, and the bride was not seen by her intended husband until the day they entered the wedding chamber as man and wife. That, as Urlai informed us, was how marriages had been performed for hundreds of years.

"I do not care what the tribe does," Jeth said. "Deborah and I will be married on the full moon, or I will carry her off into the mountain forests and have my way with her there."

"I would remind you that I am still quite strong, and you are not yet too old or big for the switch." Urlai turned to me. "Are you quite certain that you wish to marry my son?"

I suppressed a smile. "Yes, lady, I am."

There was another reason for Jeth's haste. Sisera's forces were attacking trader caravans, and the tribal leaders were meeting to decide what could be done before all trade to the towns and villages was completely cut off. When the men from the tribe of Benjamin were summoned to battle, Jeth would be among those who answered the call.

"Very well. If we are not to have a proper

betrothal—and the Lord God only knows how I will explain that away—we will have a proper wedding feast," Urlai decided. "A feast to last seven days, and no less."

I feared the expense more than the rituals involved, but Jeth assured me that everyone would contribute something of their own making, and having the feast would raise the sagging spirits of the villagers and surrounding farmers.

"We may not be able to celebrate again like this for some time," he said, and looked to the north, as he often did when he spoke of the future.

To the north lay Sisera, the general of King Jabin's armies, and the Canaanite forces that were said to be growing stronger each day.

There was much cooking and cleaning to be done to prepare for the wedding feast, and I refused to remain idle as Urlai urged. Indeed, I was happy to join in and work alongside the women of the household, for it made me feel more like one of them. Only on the Sabbath did we rest, and on that holy day, Urlai and Jeth both helped to fill in the gaps of what I did not know about the Hebrew people and their faith.

Jeth's brothers and their families arrived just as we were nearly finished preparing the food for the weeklong wedding feast, and I was formally introduced to them.

The middle brother, Imen, was big and quiet and dignified, and it did not surprise me to learn that he was, like Parah, a scribe. It also explained how Jeth could read, for his father had insisted all three boys learn.

"You are very welcome to us, sister," Imen said, gallantly bowing over my hand.

The younger brother, Syman, was shorter and more lively, but he was broader than both his larger brothers, and attributed his powerful arms and chest to the labor involved in his work as an iron-smith.

"As you see, I am short, but shaped like a brute," he told me cheerfully. "I should have gone into raising lambs or learning to make little marks on clay tablets and scrolls, but then one of my brothers would have no trade, and our tribe no decent spearheads."

"What Syman does not say is how much he liked to dally with fire too much when we were boys," Jeth said. "Once he near burnt down the barn, trying to build a fire in a brazier hot enough to melt a bit of ore he had dug up."

Imen's and Syman's wives and children altogether numbered fifteen, but each greeted
me as one of the family. It was in the midst of
this noisy brood, all trying to talk at once, that
Urlai clapped her hands together and silence
fell over her children and grandchildren.

"There, now I may hear my own thoughts."
She pointed to Jeth. "Take your brothers and
their offspring out to see the new animals. It
will give the children a chance to stretch
their legs after the long wagon ride from the
city."

The men good-naturedly herded the children out of the house, leaving me alone with
Jeth's mother and sisters-in-law.

"That is better. I vow I will enjoy growing old
and deaf, for they become noisier with each
visit." Urlai gestured to me. "Come, Deborah,
we must prepare your wedding robes and decide how to dress your hair for the ritual."

Many lengths of cloth waited in the
women's quarters, and as my knowledge of
fine garments was sadly lacking, I let Jeth's
mother and his brothers' wives decide which
should be made into my marriage clothes.
After much debate, they chose a soft
cream-colored wool, finely woven and em-

broidered with white wool thread flowers, leaves, and fruit around the collar and hems. For a sash, they selected a length of hand-knotted wool so airy and light, it appeared made of cobwebs.

The only protest I made was when Urlai sent one of the maids for her chest of jewels.

"I cannot wear jewelry," I said. "It is too much."

"It is *not* too much," she countered. "A bride on her wedding day must be the loveliest woman present. I know for a fact that every unmarried woman in the village will be attending with their families, and will adorn themselves from head to foot with every bauble they possess." She chuckled. "If only to remind Jeth of the hefty bride portions he has forsaken by not marrying them."

I knew she said this to make me feel at ease, but it reminded me that I came to this family with nothing. "I wish I had something to offer you as my portion."

"You saved my son's life in Hazor," Urlai said. At my look of surprise, she nodded. "He told me of what you did, Deborah. There is no greater gift you could have brought to this family—I assure you."

Urlai fussed greatly over which collar, bracelets, and anklets I should wear for the wedding, trying on this and that, and arguing with her sons' wives about which would flatter me best. While they were sorting through the chest, the maidservants measured me and began to sew my wedding robes from the pretty cloth. After that, I was treated to a ritual bathing to be cleansed properly. As Urlai explained, it was a custom for Hebrew women to do so before entering the temple for the marriage blessing.

I did not mind the other women seeing my naked body—it was a ritual cleansing, and part of the wedding preparation—but I wished I did not have so many ugly scars on my limbs, and that the healed wounds the whipping had left on my back were not still so pink and raw-looking.

Urlai took my hand and helped me step into the wide, flat wooden tub reserved for such special bathing. She brushed her fingers over one of the weals on the back of my shoulder.

"These are the marks of your strength and endurance, my dear," she said in a low voice. "Never feel you must hide them from us."

Unlike my courage, Urlai's kindness never failed. "I will remember, lady."

"You should practice calling me Mother." She tapped my chin and then sighed. "Here I babble on about myself without thinking of your feelings for your lady mother in heaven. If you would rather not, I shall understand."

"My mother, Dasah, would not mind, I think." I blinked back tears. "I would be proud to call you Mother."

"If you two are going to weep on each other," Syman's wife complained, "do so quickly, before the water grows cold."

The ritual cleansing took some time, as I had to be scrubbed and scraped all over, and anointed with special oils. When my body glowed, then my hair had to be washed and scented with flower essence before it was combed out and dried before the heat of a brazier, upon which myrrh and other costly resins were melted over the coals. By the time I was dressed in my robes, I smelled like a walking garden.

"You look like a queen," Urlai assured me as she braided back my smooth, scented hair. "Jeth's eyes will fall from his head when he looks upon you."

"I hope not," I said, "for I am very fond of his eyes."

"A blind husband is not the worst thing a woman can have. There, now, you look perfect." Urlai drew me up and led me over to my sleeping mat. "You will rest now, and we will bring your meals in here where you can eat in peace." She wagged a finger at me. "You cannot see Jeth until tomorrow, when we take you to meet him at the temple. It is bad luck for a bride to be seen by her husband the day before their wedding."

I agreed to stay in the women's quarters, and to take a short nap, and was left alone there. I could not sleep, however, and lay staring up at the ceiling, wondering if I had made the right choice in accepting Jeth's offer of marriage.

He is everything good and kind and decent in a man, my heart argued. *He will be a good husband.*

But would I be a good wife? Was this what Jehovah had been guiding me to, all these years? Was this why Jeth had been placed in my path, and I given the chance to save him from Ybyon's evil greed? Or was this all for different reasons, reasons that I did not wish to think upon?

The tribe had great hopes for Gesala's daughter, Urlai's voice murmured in my head, *as it was predicted that her child would become a great judge of Israel.*

I closed my eyes, and there in that beautiful room, made beautiful by the kindest women I had ever met, surrounded by luxuries I had never known, I covered my face with my hands and wept.

CHAPTER
17

I rose early the next morning and stood quietly as Urlai and her sons' wives prepared me for my wedding.

"Do not look so anxious," my new mother scolded as she reddened my lips with a bit of pomegranate juice and adjusted the hammered silver collar around my throat. "You are not, are you? No, Eleen, bring Mistress Deborah some soothing tea—that brew is too harsh."

I let my mother-in-law fuss over me. Eleen had confided in me the night before that with three sons, Urlai had never had the chance to prepare a daughter for her wedding. I was also worried that if I spoke too much, I might lose my nerve, run out to the barn, and crawl into the hay where no one could find me.

"You look perfect," Urlai finally declared, turning me this way and that. She frowned. "Smile, child. This is the beginning of your new life."

I pushed away thoughts of Gesala's legacy, and smiled.

The wedding ritual began when Jeth and his brothers brought many wagons decorated with branches of oak and bundles of wheat stalks to the front of the house to transport the family to the village temple. I was carried out of the house in a draped litter borne by four shepherds and placed in a special wagon separate from the rest of the procession, where I could not be seen. We then proceeded slowly through the village, where Jeth's kinsmen and friends lined the streets and tossed flowers and handfuls of grain as we passed before falling in behind my litter to escort us to the priest for the marriage blessing.

Urlai had explained the shower of petals and seeds were to ensure that Jeth and I had many children, but I couldn't help a pang of regret when I saw the grain fall to the ground. What was being thrown away might have been ground into flour and baked into bread, enough to feed an entire family for days. I felt better when I saw many birds swooping down to peck at it. At least it would not go entirely to waste.

The bet bama was a small shrine built on the very highest place on the plateau shared by the rest of the village. Because the community was small, it required the attendance of only a single priest, but his devotion was evident in the careful tending of the ground around the shrine, the clean look of the plastered brick, and the well-tended fires that Urlai said were never permitted to go out.

"We keep the fires burning to remind our enemies that our faith never falters," she had told me during one of the Sabbath days, when we had discussed such matters. "It is also a signal that all is well in the village."

I was handed down from the litter and escorted from the wagon by Urlai and her sons' wives. There before a four-cornered altar at the top of a stepped platform stood Jeth, dressed in magnificent dark purple robes and wearing a short, unornamented sword on his left side.

My new sisters and mother walked with

me partway up the steps, but stopped at the midpoint and urged me to continue alone. I was completely veiled, so I made my way carefully, and once I joined Jeth, he turned to the waiting priest.

"This is Deborah, late of Hazor, daughter of the tribe of Benjamin," Jeth said in his deep, steady voice. "This is whom I shall make my isti, wife."

Now it was my turn to recognize him before God. "This is Jeth, son of Lappidoth, Adon of the tribe of Benjamin," I said, trying to keep my voice as sure as his. "This is whom I shall make my isi, husband."

The priest murmured prayers and anointed both of us with oil. He then joined our hands together and bound our wrists with a golden cord.

"You are husband and wife in the eyes of Jehovah," the priest intoned. "Blessed are you in His name. May your marriage be long and fruitful, and your lives filled with the love and respect of each other and the tribe."

Jeth turned to me and removed my veil, and he looked upon my face with shining eyes. "Deborah, my wife."

I smiled up at him. How could I ever have doubted him? "Jeth, my husband."

The family, which had gathered all around the platform, called out blessings and shouted. Jeth led me down the steps, and then to the laughter and catcalls of his brothers and friends picked me up in his arms and carried me to his wagon.

"I had thought your mother and sisters were to escort me back to the house, where I would meet you at our wedding chamber," I said, glancing back at the wedding party.

"They have kept you from me for an entire day," he said, putting his arm around me. "I would like five minutes alone with my new wife."

That wagon ride back to the farm was the only time alone we had for many hours after that. Urlai and the rest of the family soon followed, as did the villagers, and all assembled around the huge tables of food set out under a grove of terebinth trees behind the house. After Urlai gave the blessing over the feast, and kissed her son and me, the celebration began.

Hebrew weddings were loud, noisy, boisterous affairs, with much singing and dancing and playing. Everyone ate as they pleased from the bounty of food prepared by Urlai and brought from the village by Jeth's kinsmen. Wine flowed freely from dozens of jugs, and cups were dipped again and again into three huge open barrels of ale.

As for Jeth and me, we were embraced and kissed and offered good wishes by every member of his family, and by so many of the villagers that I lost count of the blessings bestowed on us. Then we were ceremonially escorted to our wedding chamber, one of the bedrooms set apart from the others in the house to give a visiting couple some privacy.

Not that we were to be given any, it seemed, for Urlai had to show the room to her friends and their families to get their approval on the decorations and drapings and such. The men of the village clustered outside, making loud and often ribald suggestions to Jeth, while the women wove between them, giggling and murmuring among themselves.

The women had plagued me a bit. The older ones kept inspecting me as they might a round of lehem or a cluster of figs. The younger, who were as Urlai predicted beautifully garbed and adorned, treated me to surly or petulant glances, as if they could not believe one such as I had married the wealthiest man in their village.

I looked up at my husband and saw the mild frustration in his eyes, and felt my own match it. I stood on tiptoe to whisper against his ear, "This feast must last seven days?"

"My mother is determined to do it properly." He put his arms around me and held me there. "I knew I should have carried you off to the forest."

"There will be time for that later," someone jested, but before Jeth could respond, Imen came forward, looking grave.

"Brother, I do not wish to interrupt your celebration, but you are needed in the breeding stable." He glowered at some of the laughing men. "I do not make a joke. One of the new ewes is dropping her lamb, but it does not present its nose. She bites at anyone who comes near her."

I thought of the one pregnant ewe we had brought with us from Hazor. She was young and had a nervous disposition but was an excellent breeder.

"I know her," I said to Jeth. "She has dropped twins every year since she was first bred, and we have never lost any of her lambs. We should do what we can for her."

Urlai, who had come from the wedding chamber in time to hear Imen's message, frowned. "Go, then, and see to the animal. Only change your garments first, for you do not want to cherish your wedding robes with the stains of sheep's birthing all over them."

I went quickly to the women's quarters and changed into some ordinary garments, and met Jeth outside. He led me away to one of the barns at the very edge of the pastures, some distance from the house. Syman was waiting there by the door.

"Glad I am to see you," he hailed us. "The last time I delivered a female who snapped at me this much, my youngest son was born." He waved his hand, urging us inside. "Go, for there is much to do inside."

I did not hear the sound of a ewe in labor, and looked around the dimly lit interior of the barn. There were oil lamps lit and hung from the roof beams, but I saw no animals, only a fresh pile of hay, a neatly folded blanket, and a large covered basket.

"There is nothing to do here," I said to Jeth.

The doors slammed shut behind us, and a bolt plank was dropped. It was such a horrendous reminder of my night in the fleece shed on Ybyon's farm that I nearly screamed.

"Never fear, newly-wed," Syman called out from the other side of the door. "We thought you might wish a few hours alone, so we invented this ruse with the ewe. Imen and I will keep everyone busy at the feast while you . . . find something to do." His laughter faded as he walked away.

"We have been deceived," Jeth said, shaking his head. "Only Imen could have told such a tale with a straight face and made even my mother believe it."

My heart was still fluttering with fear and bad memories. "Your brothers are without shame. I should help your mother find her lost switch." I went over to the pile of fresh hay and examined the contents of the basket. "At least they have provided us with food and drink." I showed him the lehem, cheese, grapes, and jugs of milk and spring water inside the basket.

"I had a more comfortable setting envisioned for our first night together," my husband said, and set the basket aside. He considered the interior of the barn. "With a little effort, I think I might climb through one of the upper windows above the hay loft."

I nodded. "True. If you do not break your legs falling to the ground, you can release me, and we can return to the feast. Most of the men are in their cups, but the women will not be, and there are so many mothers who have yet to share their personal disappointment over your not choosing to wed their daughters."

"You are right." He drew me into his arms. "We will stay in here for a week."

At last, we were alone. Jeth's fingers released my hair from its intricate braid, and he spread it over my shoulders.

"I can hardly believe you are mine," he breathed, caressing my arms with the palms of his hands. "Surely this is a dream."

"My dreams come true," I reminded him, and drew his face down to mine. "So if it is, let us never wake up from it."

My wedding night was not what I had envisioned; it was so much more than I could have dreamed. Our humble surroundings dwindled away the moment Jeth touched me, and I gave myself to him with the quiet joy of one who has found the other half of her heart. In return, he taught me the ways of passion, and brought me to womanhood with the gentle tenderness that radiated from him like light from the sun.

"You *should* have carried me off into the forest," I whispered as I lay beside him on the blanket after our first time together.

He chuckled. "I am thinking I should have carried you off from the boat. Or the dock in Hazor. Or during the hailstorm." He looked down at me. "What, have you no maidenly tears?"

"I cannot cry over what we just did together. I think I might sing a bit, once I catch my breath." I laced my fingers through his. "Will we make a child tonight?"

"We will do our best," he assured me as he pulled me atop him.

Although we were both sorely tempted, we did not stay in the barn for seven days. We loved through the night, catching a little sleep here and there, and fed each other from the basket. We were lying together in contented exhaustion just after dawn, when the outer bolt was lifted and one of Jeth's shepherds walked in.

"Adon, forgive me." He stopped as soon as he saw us lying together in the hay and turned swiftly around. "I did not know you and your lady wife were here." Before either of us could speak, he made a hasty exit.

"My lady wife. I do so like the sound of

that." Jeth bent down and kissed me. "Shall I call him back to bolt us in another day?"

I checked the basket. "We will need more food."

He laughed. "So practical, my wife."

We decided to return to our wedding cele- bration before anyone woke and noticed we were gone. Jeth insisted on wrapping me in the blanket we had slept upon, although I was so warm from my night in his arms, I hardly felt the chill of the morning air.

"My mother will have something to say about this, I am sure," he warned me as we walked back to the house. "She will wish to know why we did not return to enjoy our feast."

"We have six more days of it." I looked out at the pasture where the feast tables still stood, although they were as yet bare of food. "I cannot fathom how people can eat so much and not throw up. It astonished me yesterday as I watched them go at the food."

"Most drink too much and fall insensible before their bellies are overfull," my husband said, and nodded to an older man who was rushing from the house and into some brush. The sounds that followed were unmis- takably those of retching. "They still pay for their excesses the next morning."

Urlai was already awake and working with her maidservants to prepare the morning meal in the kitchen. From the enormous amount of bread, fruit, and stew they were placing on platters, I wondered if the entire village was to show up to break their fast.

"Ah, look, Eleen, it is my beautiful new daughter, and my highly disrespectful, ungrateful son." Urlai picked up a pot of tea and waved us over to the table. "Come, sit. Tell me of this imaginary ewe and the lamb she was not birthing last night."

"How do you manage to know everything before I can get out a single word of explanation or apology?" Jeth asked.

"I have not always been old and widowed, my son. Besides, you both have hay in your hair. Somehow I doubt you delivered this ewe while standing on your heads." She set out cups for us and filled them with a fragrant tea. "It is your brother Imen who will apologize and make penance for telling a falsehood." She put a platter of food on the table. "Now, eat."

We ate while Urlai chattered on about some of the antics we had missed at last night's feasting.

"The village wheelwright drank enough wine to convince himself he would finally win a wrestling match against your younger brother, and so challenged his manhood," my mother-in-law said. "Syman had him pinned by the count of three and back on his feet and shaking his hand and laughing by the count of ten."

"Syman could thrash a Canaanite, and then charm him into giving him his married daughters," Jeth said, rolling his eyes.

"Your brother who cannot tell the truth to his mother tells me that the word came down from the tabernacle and has spread through the cities to the north. The judge and the general of prophecy will be with us within the moon." Urlai turned to me. "I never asked you, my dear, but have you any brothers by your mother?"

"Not that I am aware." I had sometimes wondered if Meji might be my mother's son, but as we grew up his skin had darkened so much that I thought him instead partly of Egyptian descent. He also had looked nothing like me.

"A pity." Urlai frowned at our plates. "Why are you not eating? Deborah, do you wish to starve my grandson?"

My jaw sagged, and then I looked at my husband.

"Mother, we cannot know if there is to be a child for some weeks," Jeth said reasonably.

"As tired as you both look?" My mother-in-law chuckled. "It shall not take that long."

Our wedding feast did last six more days, although after the first night, Jeth and I did not have to sneak away to the barn for more time alone together. Every night we were escorted to the wedding chamber by our guests, but then left there alone together until dawn.

During the days of our wedding feast, there was much eating and drinking and merriment, but that was not all. Each of the villagers brought some special dish for Jeth and me to try, and I learned more about the foods beloved by my mother's people. Our kinsmen also contributed some fine entertainment to the celebration. There were many gifted singers among Jeth's kinsmen, and they treated us to a variety of songs, from solemn arias of praise to the One and True God to funny, often scandalous songs about life in the country and on the farm.

Some of the older children put on a little play and acted out the story of Moses freeing the Hebrew people from Pharaoh and slavery in Egypt. The play came complete with realistic enactments of the plagues Jehovah sent down on the cruel Pharaoh, and Urlai balked only at allowing the grasshoppers the children had caught to be set loose.

"Keep them in their cages, and we will imagine them flying into our hair and food," she said firmly.

A few of the women danced, and taught me one of the group dances they performed during special holy days. I was not so surefooted as they, so the results made me laugh as much as our audience. The men demonstrated feats of strength, dexterity, and accuracy, and even the wheelwright won back respect from his neighbors by showing how steady his hands were when he was sober by balancing a goblet full of wine on the tip of one finger.

I had never enjoyed myself so, and on the last day of the feast, I was almost sorry it was over. But by the time the villagers had bestowed their last gifts and blessings, Urlai was so exhausted that she retired to the house, followed by her drooping maidservants, leaving me and Jeth to bid farewell to Syman and Imen and their families.

"We will return in the spring if the roads are safe," Imen promised us. He kissed my cheek and clasped Jeth's hands. "Send word if you need us before then."

I had noticed how careful the men were during the feast not to speak of the problems outside the settlement, but Imen's discreet comment made me wonder just how soon we would be facing a war with the Canaanites.

Syman kissed my mouth boldly, and then cuffed Jeth's shoulder when he uttered a jealous growl. "You deserve better than my overlarge bucolic brother, beautiful Deborah, but I suppose the other women of the land will be grateful to you for saving them the trouble. I love you both dearly. Look after our mother for us."

As soon as we returned inside, I sought out my mother-in-law and found her dozing by the workroom fire. I put my arm around her shoulders and urged her to her feet.

"Ah, Deborah." She smothered a yawn. "Have the boys gone home? I should see to the evening meal."

"I shall cook it," I told her as I steered her toward the women's quarters, "and bring it to you, if I do not burn it and you are still awake." I had my doubts on both accounts.

"That I shall not be." She smiled at me, apparently too tired to argue. "You are a good daughter already."

I gave the household staff instructions to eat if they wished and then to go straight to bed, and not to let me see them until the sun was up. They happily obeyed me.

I saw my new husband observed all this with silent amusement. "You, Adon, may join me in the kitchen."

"I may?" His eyebrows rose.

"Someone must eat the first meal I cook by myself," I said. "If it does not make you sick, then I will know it is safe to cook for the others."

Although I had learned much in the kitchen during the feast, I was still not so accomplished a cook as Urlai, or as skillful as Eleen. Thus I managed a passable broth and some uneven but tasty lehem. Jeth and I sat together at the little table in the kitchen and shared the meal between us.

I noticed him tasting the broth with caution. "I was only jesting. I stopped making people sick with my food many days past."

"It is ambrosia," Jeth assured me after one sip. "I have never tasted better."

I dipped a piece of bread in the bowl. "It needs more garlic, and you need not soothe my pride." I studied the bread I had baked. "How does your mother make it come out of the oven so round?"

"I believe the oven is afraid of her," Jeth said gravely. "It would not dare produce anything but perfect loaves."

"Hmmm." I tore off another lopsided chunk. "I will work on browbeating the oven, then."

The wedding feast and having so many with us had been a delight, but I was happy to have my husband to myself. After our meal, we went directly to our wedding chamber, which we had already decided would be our sleeping chamber after the feasting was over.

"You must be tired," Jeth said as I closed the door and slipped out of my robe.

I went to him, and hooked my arms around his waist. "Are you?"

He smiled. "The moment I step through that door, I cannot think of sleeping—but I have not let you have many hours of rest, wife."

"I shall rest when we are old, husband," I promised him, and drew him down to our sleeping mat.

Later I must have fallen asleep in his

arms, for I went from the sweet warmth of his kiss into a chilly place where there was no form or light.

"It is time to choose, Truth-seer," a rough, familiar voice said. "Which path will you take?"

I could not see the warrior of the black cloak, or the sword he carried, but I could feel him there. I could also feel the darkness dividing itself within me, split in half as the sky had been by an invisible bolt of lightning.

"Must I choose now?" I asked. "I am only just married. I have a husband, a family now. Give me more time, please."

"The time is now, and the choice must be made."

I could not choose without seeing, and so I looked into my own truth for the first time.

Like my mother, I was made for the path of flowers. I was not perfect, a child of dream gardens and fountains of water I had never tasted, but my heart was warm and open, and I could still love. I could be a wonderful wife to Jeth and devoted daughter to Urlai, and become a loving mother to the many children I wished to have with my husband.

It was wrenching to look beyond those sweet, peaceful desires and into the core of my soul. The way there was not strewn with petals but with sharpedged stone. It bruised me to go there, to see what my life had fashioned of me. Beyond the soft and sweet was a terrible place of hunger and pain and loss. There a part of me dwelt, still and watchful, unable to lie, unable to look away. There my heart lay open to God's will alone.

Nothing else mattered but God's will.

I came out of myself slowly, and found I was standing on the empty green plain with the strange warrior. Only he was no longer unknown to me.

"Son of Kedesh." I rested my left hand upon his brow, and he closed his eyes. I opened myself to Jehovah, and felt his will pour through me. "This is the word of your Lord God. You will leave Naphtali this day. You will journey to the south, to Ephraim, to me."

"How will I know you?" he asked.

"I am the last of Ehud's blood," I told him, flinching as that truth came from my lips. "I am the judge of Israel, and the seer of truth. Know me by my name: Deborah, wife of Lappidoth."

Barak went down on one knee and touched the hem of my robe. "So be it, Deborah."

I came awake with a silent scream locked

in my throat. Beside me, my husband slept, unaware of my dream. I rose, careful not to disturb him, and slipped out of our chamber. I went to the kitchen to fetch some water for my sore throat, but when I lifted the dipper from the jug, I saw my reflection, and nearly spilled the water down the front of myself. I lifted a tress of my hair and saw the proof spread over my fingers.

The hair at my temples had gone completely white.

CHAPTER
18

"I have seen women grow suddenly old and tired after birthing too many children too close together, but this?" Urlai touched a strand of my hair. "It is not the silver of age, either. Look, Jeth. It is not a dye or some sort of soiling. It truly has gone white, like snow."

"Deborah has endured much since I brought her here to meet you," my husband said, sounding unconcerned. "I would not be surprised if she woke up with all her hair white tomorrow morning."

"Hmmm." Urlai eyed me as I picked up a jug of water. "Passing strangers would think her my younger sister, not my new daughter.

Only you are still too young-looking, Jeth. Perhaps I will give you both more grief."

I could not join in their usual jesting with each other, even when I was the target of their jokes. During the night I had walked the floors for hours, trying to fathom the terrible dream, and what I had done by choosing the path of stones and pain instead of the way of flowers.

"Child. *Child.*"

I looked down and saw that I had poured so much water into my cup that it was overflowing. Quickly I set down the jug and rose to fetch a cloth.

"No, stay where you are." Urlai retrieved the cloth and mopped up the mess. "I should not tease you so. It must have worried you to see your hair changed overnight, and I am not making it any better, am I?"

"I was not expecting it." I looked at my husband. "Do you know of a warrior in a northern tribe by the name of Barak?"

"Barak is a tribal leader from Kedesh. He fought bravely in the border skirmishes with Jabin's troops, and saved many villages from being burned by placing watchers in the mountains." He gave me a curious look. "How do you know his name? Did you hear of him in Hazor? I would not think Jabin would be reckless enough to let him near the town."

"No. I . . . it matters not." I rose awkwardly. "I must go to the priest in the village this morning. How can I do that?"

"I will take you to the bet bama." Jeth came around the table and took my cold hands in his. "What is it? All the color is gone from your face."

"I must see the priest," I said. "I cannot explain until I speak to him."

"I hope you do not already wish to divorce my son," Urlai complained, and then peered at me. "Jeth, something is wrong. I can see it in her eyes. Hitch up the wagon and take her, right away."

I knew I was frightening both of them, but I could not speak openly of what I had dreamed. Some part of me knew that only a priest of Jehovah could advise me what would be the next step along the path I had chosen.

Jeth drove me in silence into the village, and walked with me to the holy place where only eight days ago our marriage had been blessed. "Do you wish me to go in with you? The priest is an old friend."

"No. You must stay here." I saw the shadow of fear in his eyes, and took a moment to embrace him. "Trust me as you love me, husband, for I cannot yet explain this. Not until I speak with the holy one."

He nodded and released me.

The bet bama's altar was outside the building of the shrine, in the open air where offerings could be burned and the smoke would rise unto heaven. Within the shrine were two large, flat stones into which footsteps had been carved to symbolize the silent steps of the Lord God among us. Beyond them were the many smaller altars where various weekly offerings were made, and a portent table where the priest would read signs for those seeking guidance.

The elderly man who had recited our marriage blessing appeared as soon as I crossed the threshold.

"Lady Deborah," he greeted me. "I was expecting you." He gestured toward one of the chairs by the portent table and sat across from me there.

"Priest, I must know what to do now." I tried to think of how to begin. "I am not what I seem."

He smiled a little. "I knew that from the

moment you arrived in this village. You already know what you must do, lady. It is clear from the touch of Jehovah"—he gestured to my white wings of hair—"that you have made your choice."

It was then that I saw he, too, had the same white streaks in his silver-gray hair. "You are a truth-seer like me?"

"Alas, no, lady. My kind are called guides. We are like the herd dog that keeps the sheep from straying—we follow the word. We do not deliver it." He covered my hand with his. "You, lady, are a fountain of truth. I saw that the day I married you to Jeth. You shall be a powerful judge of Israel."

"They will never believe that of me. They cannot name me a judge. I am only a woman." I swallowed hard. "In Hazor, I was a slave."

"Those Jehovah raises up are often of humble beginning. Such as the one you summoned." He nodded toward the north. "He comes from Kedesh, at your command. He travels quickly."

I had my own moment of doubt. "How could you know that?"

"Guides always know. The Lord God made it known to us last night, through our dreams. Now you come seeking the next step along the difficult path." His eyes met mine, and for a moment it was as if he looked into my soul. "It is this: You must make yourself known to the tribal elders before he arrives, for they alone can give him the men he needs for our army."

If I had any doubt of the truth of my dreams, or the existence of our God, it was now banished forever. "Do they not know what is coming?"

He sighed and patted my hand. "Tribal leaders are chosen by men, to rule men. They know little more than their own ambition. You must not go alone."

I drew back, still reluctant. "I have not even told my husband of this. I cannot think how to. Now I must ask him to take me to these men?"

The priest cocked his head much like one of the herd dogs. "You have no time to ask, and you cannot lie to him. You cannot remain silent in the days to come. The most convincing way is to have him go with you to see the tribal leaders. Let him see, as they must, why you have come to us. It is not the path of flowers, Deborah. You knew this last night."

"Yes." I bent down and pressed my brow

to the back of his hand. "I thank you for guiding me, Holy One. I will do what I can to follow your wisdom."

An old hand touched the back of my head. "Jehovah walks with you, Truth-seer. Trust in Him."

I walked out of the shrine and saw Jeth pacing at the base of the platform. At the sound of my footsteps, he looked up, visibly relieved to see me emerge.

"All is well, then." He came to help me down the steps. "We shall go home and you may rest. I will order my mother to cease her teasing of you."

"We shall not go home," I told him. "I must travel now to where the tribal leaders are meeting. Do you know this place?"

"The meeting place in Rameh? Of course. But why? Why go there now?" He seemed completely bewildered.

"I bring a message for them, husband." I turned away from him. "You will drive me there?"

He glanced back toward the farm. "We must stop back at the house to gather supplies and food for the journey—"

"There is no time. If you will not drive me

there now, I will do it myself." I climbed up onto the wagon seat.

The priest came out of the shrine and walked down to where Jeth stood staring at me.

"What did you say to her?" he demanded of the old man.

"Only what she needed to hear. Go with her, my son," the priest said. "She will need you when she is done with them."

The journey to Rameh was long, cold, and uncomfortable. I sat in silence beside my husband, willing him to trust in me, praying that our marriage would stand this, the first of many trials to come.

Halfway down the mountain road, Jeth said, "I have known the village priest since I was a boy. He has always attended my family, and trusts me without reservation, I believe. He has known you but a few days, knows nothing of your past or your kin, and yet he sides with you against me. What did you say to him when you were in there?"

"There is one side in this," I said tonelessly. "It is not yours or mine. It is the side of God."

"You are frightening me, wife."

I knew I was, so I held my tongue for the remainder of the journey. We reached Rameh just before nightfall, and Jeth drove the wagon to a stable near the place where the tribal leaders had gathered.

"I would go to one of my brothers' homes, but I fear our sudden appearance would alarm them. Can we hire a room at an inn?" He put his warm hand to my cold face. "Truly, Deborah, you look very pale now, and you have had nothing to eat. Let me order food and have them build a fire—"

"No." I climbed down from the wagon. "If you will not take me to them, tell me how to go there."

"It was only a suggestion." He took my stiff hand in his and led me from the stable.

The dwelling where the tribal leaders had gathered belonged to one of the most important merchants in the town, who Jeth told me had given up his residence temporarily to give the men the space they needed. We were met at the door by an armed guard.

"What do you wish?" the guard asked.

"I carry a message for the leaders," I told him. When he held out his hand, I shook my head. "It is not that sort of message."

The guard's hand went to his sword. "Who are you, and what manner of fool entrusts a woman with a message for our leaders?"

I seized his wrist in my hand and felt something flow from me into him. "You will take me to them."

"Yes, lady. This way." The guard meekly turned, and we followed him inside.

"How did you do that?" my husband murmured to me.

"I did nothing." I looked ahead into a large chamber, where many men in fine robes were gathered around the remains of a meal. The tribal leaders of the Hebrews were important men, judging by the garments, but they were not eating well. Food lay neglected all over the tables and on their plates.

"A messenger, Adoni," the guard announced.

I walked in, but the men's eyes went to my husband behind me.

"What message do you bring, Jeth, son of Lappidoth?" one of the men who recognized my husband asked.

"I regret to say that I bring only the messenger." He gestured to me. "My wife, Deborah."

Some of the men chuckled, while others frowned. One elderly leader rose to his feet to address me. "You have word for us from a kinsman, wife of Lappidoth?"

"I bring the word of the Lord God Jehovah," I said in a clear, strong voice. "Hear me, men of Israel, for your time of waiting and suffering is at an end."

Nearly all the men laughed at this, and I felt Jeth stiffen beside me. I could offer him no comfort, nor could I berate the men for their disrespect. Neither served my purpose, which had to be met here and now.

The elderly leader did not find my words amusing, but he did move forward and stare hard at me. "Who are you, woman, and how dare you speak of the word of God?"

"I am Deborah, daughter of Gesala," I said, and ignored the gasps that raced around the room. "Granddaughter of Ehud, and the last of his line. The Lord your God has sent me to you to speak His will."

The elderly leader was now standing before me, his eyes narrow and suspicious. "You are lying. Gesala was killed as a child in Ephraim."

Without warning I put my left hand upon his brow. I felt him flinch, then go still under my touch.

"You know yourself that she was not,

Dareus of Megiddo," I said as the dream came over me. "You had the confession of her abduction and enslavement from a raider you caught on your land. He confessed to his part in the raid that killed her father and uncles, and snatched her from the tribe. He hoped it would entice you to spare his life. Instead, you slew him and kept the secret to yourself. You were a young and ambitious leader in those days, and you feared the coming of another leader who might take your power from you: Gesala's child."

Dareus staggered back, stunned and speechless.

I looked at the men who were no longer laughing. "Who else wishes to know the truth? I will speak it for you. I will see it in you."

The men exchanged glances, and one came to lead Dareus away from me. No one spoke.

"Do you all fear a mere woman?" Jeth asked softly. "You were eager to laugh at her. Have none of you the spine to stand her touch?"

"No man wishes to challenge a lady," one of the younger tribesmen said, "but I have nothing to hide." He strode over to stand before me. "See into me, woman, and if what you discover is true, then I will listen to your message."

I grasped his wrist. "Eru, son of Bora, tribal leader of Rameh, and his second wife, Coran. You do not hide, but you have kept silent and let others believe something that is not true. The men here think you come to sit as leader while your father is away, but he is here in this town, abed and dying. You go to him every night instead of sleeping to hold council with what has been said. You lied because he instructed you to, so that you could be his eyes and ears while his are failing. You are a devoted son, but you should not fear your father's death. He goes to a better place before the new moon, and you will be made leader in his stead."

Eru's eyes closed for a moment. "May it be so." He looked back at the other men. "She speaks the truth. My father is not in the hill country, as you have thought. He has the wasting sickness and is home now, with my mother caring for him."

The room fell silent as Eru took his place among the leaders. The men seemed not to know what to do.

At last Dareus spoke in a withered voice. "I always knew you would come. I have had bad dreams about killing that raider and keeping my silence all these years. Speak, then, Gesala's daughter, and tell us of the punishment Jehovah intends to visit upon our people."

"Not a punishment, Dareus, but a champion. He comes journeying from the far north country, even now as I speak to you. He is coming, and nothing will stop him." I looked into the elderly man's sad eyes. "He is the leader you have been awaiting, brought up by Jehovah to lead us to victory as my grandfather was eighty years ago. His name is Barak of Kedesh."

"I know of this man," Jeth said, "and so must many of you. He is a dedicated warrior with many years of experience."

"When this Barak arrives, how will he banish King Jabin's armies from our land?" one man sneered. "By the word of Jehovah? Or by his will alone? Or does your woman mean to give him some of her power?"

"You will give Barak the means by readying forces for him to lead against Sisera and his armies," I told them. "He will need twenty thousand men, armed and ready, to journey to Ephraim within the week. You will provide him with these men."

Many of the leaders made sounds of disbelief, but Dareus called for silence.

"Lady," he pleaded, "twenty thousand are all the battle-experienced men we have."

"The Lord God has commanded you, Dareus. If Barak does not have these men at ready, we will lose this land to Sisera and his forces, and our people will die under their swords. For whether or not you are ready to go to war, they are coming for us." The power sizzling through me ebbed, and I sagged back against Jeth. "Take me away from here now, husband. Take me home."

Jeth put an arm around me and led me from the room. As we walked out of the house, young Eru appeared and stopped us.

"Dareus has commanded the tribes to make their men ready for this Barak. I go now to my father, but I will advise him to do the same." He peered at me. "You truly are the last of Ehud's line?"

"She is," Jeth said, his tone one of warning, "and exhausted now, so please step aside and let us pass."

"I wish only to express my gratitude for your lady seeing the end of my father's suffering," Eru said urgently. "My mother and I have long worried that he might linger in agony for months, as some do with this sickness. It will be a comfort to him to know he is going home soon, and for that I thank you, Lady Deborah." He tried to smile at Jeth. "You are surely blessed. Do you need an escort back to Ephraim? I can provide you men."

"I thank you, no," Jeth said. "We will spend the night at an inn, and go back in the morning, when the roads are safer."

"Then Jehovah watch over you both," Eru said, and bowed before hurrying off.

The inn at which Jeth found a room for us was little better than Dhiban's had been in Hazor. I was too weary to care, however, and barely made it to the sleeping mat before I collapsed.

"Does seeing like this always exhaust you so?" Jeth said as he covered me with a blanket the innkeeper had given him.

"It is easier to sleep and dream than to summon a waking dream," I told him. His expression was still closed, and I wished desperately that I could make the last day vanish. "Forgive me for my demanding manner, but after last night, I know I am no longer free to do as I wish. I must see this through, and there will not be time for explanations and pretty words."

"Why did you not at least tell me that this was a holy matter?" he asked me. "You had me wondering if you had gone mad."

"I knew you would doubt my words if I spoke of seeing this, so I had to show you." I rubbed my eyes. "Just as I had to show them."

"Next time, trust me enough to tell me, and I vow I will believe you." He stretched out before me and pulled me against his chest, tucking my head under his chin. "I am your husband now, Deborah. We must share our burdens. Will you try to do that for me?"

I nodded.

"Good." He kissed the top of my head. "Now sleep. In the morning, we shall go home."

CHAPTER
19

Jeth roused me just after dawn to make the return journey to Ephraim. He obtained a bundle of food from somewhere in town for us, but I felt too tired and worried to eat much of it.

"Do you know when Barak will arrive?" he asked me as we left Rameh.

"Soon. Before the Sabbath. He will come to the farm alone, at midday." I thought of Jeth's mother and groaned. "With us gone and no word, Urlai will be so worried. Forgive me."

"I suspect the priest went to see my mother and told her of our leaving," my husband said. "If he did not, she will surely go to him." He pushed a wedge of bread and a raisin cake into my hands. "If you grow thin, she will nag me for not taking better care of you."

My face grew hot. "It is my duty to care for you, and I have made a poor job of it."

Jeth stopped the wagon and turned to me. "There is more coming ahead. You do not say, but there must be. Perhaps Jehovah brought us together so that I could care for you while you do His work."

I looked at the food in my hands. Only two moons past would I have been overjoyed to have such fare. "You are not angry with me?"

"How can I be? You have done no wrong. Indeed, I think you are but an instrument of the Lord." He put his arm around me. "I may be selfish enough to wish He had put this burden on the shoulders of another man's wife, but I love you, and it pains me to see you suffer."

"I chose my burden," I admitted. "I did not have to do this. It is my will as well as His." I looked up into his kind, handsome face. "I did ask for more time for us, but it was not to be. Events are moving quickly, and if we are not ready . . ." I did not wish to think of what would happen to Israel if Barak and I failed to carry out our mission.

"I shall do whatever I can to help," Jeth promised, and slapped the reins on the oxen's broad backs. "You have only to say."

I nodded and lifted the raisin cake to my lips, forcing myself to eat.

Urlai met us at the farm road, where evidently she had been waiting and watching. Jeth helped her up to sit beside me, and drove on to the house. My mother-in-law embraced me without a word and held me in her arms until we stopped again.

"All is well," she told Jeth. "The shepherds are tending to the animals, and they tell me one of the new ewes delivered twins last night with no difficulty." Urlai climbed down and held out her hand to me. "Come, Deborah. Come inside now."

I went in with my mother-in-law as Jeth drove on to the stables. She had hot food waiting, and gently bullied me into drinking some soup.

"The priest came down after you left Palma yesterday to tell me of your journey to Rameh." She sighed. "I confess I was quite upset at first. In my anger, I may have said some foolish things. The holy one forgave me, of course, but I will have to make a proper offering and ask His forgiveness." She hesitated for a moment. "It is true, then? You have seen the one who will lead our armies?"

I nodded. "He comes to me even now to receive the word of God." I leaned my brow against my palm. "Sisera comes, too. His armies are only a few days hence." I closed my eyes. "If they are not stopped, they will destroy everything in their path."

"Then you do whatever is needed, my daughter." Urlai's hand stroked over my hair. "For this you were born, and for this you were brought back to us."

I prayed she was right, for if I had made the wrong choice, my mistake would cost our people everything.

I had only a few days to ready myself for Barak's coming, and in an eerie sense it was much like preparing for my wedding—except now there would be no feast, and no celebrating.

Israel was going to war.

After three tense days, when I expected the warrior from the north to appear at any moment, my mother-in-law suggested I undergo another ritual cleansing, to which I agreed. She summoned some of the older women from the village to help. They prayed together over me as I was bathed, and stayed to offer comfort. Many were old enough to remember Gesala, and told their stories about her.

"Ehud's daughter was the kindest of women," the weaver's wife said. "She came to my mother when my brother Shami was only a babe, and although he was the smallest and weakest of her sons, she gave Mother hope. We were poor, and so I did not altogether believe her when she said that my brother would grow to become a strong and important man. Years passed, and Shami was among those who established the eastern trade routes. Shami grew to be taller and broader than any of our brothers, and wealthy enough to marry a merchant's daughter. Today he provides for our widowed mother and poor kinfolk, as well as for his own wife and seven children."

"So it was with my older sister's husband," the potter's wife said. "Gesala warned my brother-in-law not to travel into Taanach when the weather was fair and all seemed well for the journey. He heeded her words, thank Jehovah, and a few hours later a sudden storm rose in the east. That day two caravans were lost when floodwaters washed out the road."

Eleen came into the women's quarters. "Lady Urlai, there is a man at the door asking to see the master."

"I will speak to him." My mother-in-law had seen me flinch, and she touched my shoulder. "Likely it is only a trader or one of the men from the village."

I knew from the cold shiver that passed through me that it was not, but I waited until Urlai had gone before I excused myself and followed her.

The room where visitors were received at the front of the house had two entryways, both hung with airy curtains of wooden beads, and I stood outside one to listen to the voices of Urlai and the visitor.

"I have come to see the truth-seer," the voice that had haunted my terrible dreams was saying to Urlai. "You will fetch him to me."

"Do I look like a servant to you, Adon?" my mother-in-law snapped. "For I assure you, I am not."

"Then send one of your girls," the man

said reasonably. "But I am not leaving until I speak with him."

Urlai sighed. "My son is a farmer, and while he tries always to see the truth, he is not the one who . . . sent for you."

Wooden beads rattled as I stepped through the entry curtain. "I am the one who summoned you."

He stood, straight as an oak, and looked into my eyes. His were black as night, and harder to fathom. Although I knew the sky outside to be clear and bright, I heard a distant rumble of thunder, and suppressed a shudder.

"I am sent by the One and True God," he said simply. "I am Barak, leader of Kedesh."

I did not want to speak to this man. I wanted to run out of the room and call for Jeth, and hide until my husband made him leave. Even as those cowardly thoughts formed, I saw my hand move and heard my mouth say, "Sit down, please."

We sat at the table facing each other, and I waited for him to speak. He took a few moments to study me, and I knew his sharp eyes took in every detail of my countenance.

"You have white in your hair, but you are

so young." It seemed to confuse him. For a moment the man I had seen in my dreams studied me. "*You* are the truth-seer. A woman."

"Perhaps my son should have a word with you," Urlai, who was hovering behind me, said. Her eyes went bright with ire. "I will summon Jeth."

"Yes, Mother, I think that would be wise. I will entertain General Barak until my husband comes."

"I am not a general," Barak said.

"Not yet," I agreed. I saw Urlai speak to Eleen, who hurried off, but my mother-in-law lingered at the door as if reluctant to leave me alone with the stranger. "Mother, our visitor seems tired after his long journey. Perhaps you could arrange some refreshment for him?"

Reminded of her duties as hostess, Urlai nodded and went off toward the kitchens.

"You are Deborah, wife of Lappidoth?" Barak asked me.

"I am." I could see that he was not a young man, perhaps some ten years older than me, and his face and arms showed the scars of battle and a life spent fighting in the hot sun. His path had been much harder than mine, so it was easy to understand his suspicion. "You have been dreaming of me."

"I have." He seemed uncomfortable admitting so. "I woke with your name on my lips six days past, and knew only that I had to come here." His dark brows drew together. "I left behind my family, my brothers, everything I have to come here. But it cannot be for you. There is a mistake."

"You would trust in the vision sent to you by our Lord enough to make such a journey, but deny that a woman could be the one you seek?" I wondered if Jehovah had made the right choice in this man. "You were chosen for the strength of your faith, Barak, as well as your experience at war."

"Why were you chosen?"

"I am the granddaughter of Ehud." I saw the shock of that cross his features like a flicker of light. "And a woman. And just married. And, until recently, a slave to a Canaanite in Hazor." I folded my arms. "Imagine for a moment how it is to walk *my* path."

"However much I despise King Jabin and the Canaanites, I cannot begin a war on the word of a woman," Barak argued. "Even if you are as you say the last of Ehud's line, you have no experience of such things."

"I am only the messenger, Adon," I reminded him. "The word is that of Jehovah."

He paced the length of the room. "I knew this was madness. My wife tried to persuade me to reason, but I could not resist the call of the dream. It was as if I had been possessed by demons. Now I must listen to you to make war on the Canaanites."

"When I went to trade in Hazor, I met Deborah there," Jeth said as he came into the room to stand beside me. "She was a slave to an evil man who abused Hebrews, and learned he intended to slay me. Like you, I did not believe her word at first. But she risked her life to warn me, and saved my life by convincing me to listen. Do you know what was her payment?"

Barak gave my husband a hard look. "You were so grateful that you married her?"

"No, I married her because I love her. You may look upon the cost of that truth." With a gentle hand my husband turned me so that my back was to Barak, and pushed the loose collar of my robe down far enough to expose the lash marks at the top of my spine. "The scars reach down to her hips."

"How was this done to her?" Barak asked in a low, disgusted tone.

"She was tied to a tree and whipped," my husband said. "They had nearly beaten her to death before I could get to her."

Barak moved closer, as if to examine the whip marks. "This happened on the full moon two months past?" Jeth nodded. "I felt it. There was a night in that time that I woke from a terrible nightmare, my back afire. The pain did not go away for many days. I could barely move."

"There is a reason for that, as well," I said, shrugging my robe back into place and facing him. I did not have to touch him, for I saw the truth in his face. "Your mother is a Hebrew, but your father was a Canaanite."

Now Barak looked astonished. "How could you know that?"

I grasped his wrist. "Barak, son of Lena, maidservant in the house of a Canaanite trader. Lena, who was violated by one of her master's guests. She returned to her family, and they arranged a marriage to cover what had been done to her." I released him and met his horrified gaze. "You felt my pain because we share the same father, Barak. You are my half brother."

I thought for a moment he might raise his hand to me. After touching him, I knew that he had the same capacity for brutality as Ybyon. But Barak had been raised by his gentle mother, who had never faulted him for the sins of our father. It was she who had tamed the anger within him and shaped him into the warrior who sought justice, not revenge.

The proud warrior fell to his knees and bowed his head. "I submit myself to you, last of Ehud's line, Truth-seer, Judge of Israel." He looked up. "I will do as you wish."

I stared at the cropped silver-black of his hair before I held out my hand to him. "Then rise, brother, and call me Deborah."

We had been speaking for only a few moments when my mother-in-law and two servants came with tea, cheese, fruit and lehem. The repast was generous, and I gave Urlai a smile of gratitude.

"I am glad Jeth is here," she murmured to me. "Do you wish me to stay?"

"No, Mother. All will be well."

With one final suspicious look at Barak, Urlai herded the servants out of the room and closed the door.

"She is very protective of you," Barak said.

I poured a cup of tea for him. "She is a good mother." I sat back and let the men talk of trade routes and travel until the meal was finished.

"I must go and tend to my flocks," Jeth said, rising from his chair. "Barak, you are welcome to stay with us for as long as you wish." He bent over and kissed my cheek. "If you need me, send for me."

Barak watched my husband go. "He seems a good man."

"He is." I studied my brother's face. "Our father was made to pay for the evil he has caused so many. King Jabin seized his property and had him sold into slavery."

"I have always wished to know of him," Barak admitted. "Each time I fought Canaanites, I wondered if I might be crossing blades with my own father." He went to look out the window. "So I am here, sister, and I am in your hands. I have been dreaming for weeks of a coming battle. Jehovah showed me my men littering the ground, their blood turning the sand crimson. He said if I did not follow the Truth-seer's word that this would be the outcome."

I stood and held out my hands. "Come, then, and I will deliver the word to you."

He came, and took my hands in his.

I closed my eyes and summoned the waking dream. "The Lord God has commanded you, Barak of Kedesh. Now you will summon ten thousand of the tribes from Naphtali and Zebulun, and go to Mount Tabor, and meet you there the ten thousand men of the southern tribes. There shall be drawn to the river Kishon the enemy, Sisera, commander of Jabin's army, with his chariots and his multitude. Do this, and I will deliver him into your hands."

"I may be able to raise ten thousand from the northern tribes," Barak said as soon as I released him. "But the southern leaders do not know me, and they will give me nothing."

I groped for a chair and dropped down onto it. "I have already spoken to our tribal leaders in Rameh some days past. As we speak, they are readying their men. They know you have been chosen to lead them."

"And I am to lead twenty thousand men to Mount Tabor, and wait there for Sisera to attack?" He shook his head. "This is not a sound battle plan. I know that land. The plains around the mountain are open and provide no cover. Sisera has a thousand chariots under his command. The only retreat is into a swamp by the Kishon."

"You are not to occupy the plains or the

swamp. You are to climb the mountain and maintain a defense position there," I told him, leaning back and willing myself to stay awake. "The southern troops will arrive, and at a sign from Jehovah, we will send down a diversion, and draw them away to the Kishon, where the final battle will happen."

"I cannot understand this," he said, making a frustrated gesture. "I am to begin a war by hiding from our enemies on a mountain, and then leading them *away* from it? How may I do that if we are on the mountain? What is this sign from Jehovah? What diversion do we use?"

"I do not yet know all the details." I rubbed my eyelids. "He will make them known to me when it is time."

"So we go to war without knowing what we are to do, until you are told." Barak began pacing again. "Are you certain this is *God* telling you these things?"

"Sisera will meet defeat at the Kishon," I told him. "It is God's will."

"Very well. If we must all die to serve Jehovah's purpose, then so be it." My brother took hold of my wrist this time and stared down at me. "But I shall not lead men to their deaths by myself. If you will go with me, then

I will go, but if you will not go with me, then I will not go."

Jeth found me sitting in the lambing pen some time later, a little newborn ewe on my lap. "Deborah."

"I have missed caring for these little ones. They are so beautiful and perfect when they are small, and in need of so much affection." I looked up at him and saw the bleakness in his face. "Barak has told you we are leaving today."

My husband climbed over the fence and came to sit with me. "I will go with you. I need only a few minutes to tell Urlai and give my shepherds instructions on what to do while I am gone."

"You cannot. You are needed here, and there will doubtless be skirmishes around the towns and villages. The people here are sending most of their men to war. Someone must stay behind, and it is you." I moved the sleepy lamb onto a soft pile of dried grass and turned to Jeth, curling my arms around his neck. "I will be gone until the war is over."

"Is there no other way?"

I shook my head. "Barak can lead and fight, but to win, he needs to see beyond what can be seen. Only I can do that for him." I sighed. "He regards me as a sister now. He will care for me."

"Not as a husband would." Jeth pressed me close. "What will I do if you never return? How can I continue without you, beloved?"

"We will never be apart here." I placed my hand over the strong beat of his heart. "If the worst happens, then know that I am waiting for you in the kingdom of heaven."

Urlai had garments and food packed for the journey by the time Jeth and I walked back to the house. She did not bother to conceal the fact that she had been weeping, or that my second abrupt departure disturbed her.

"I am calling for the holy one again, and I will have him explain to me why a young woman must go to war and leave behind her husband and those who love her." She instructed the maidservants to take the food baskets out to Barak's pack animals. "This newfound brother of yours is waiting outside. I have already told him what I will do to him if you are not returned to us. He has no manners to speak of—do they raise nothing but barbarians in the north country? Ah, well, it matters not. Is there anything else I may do?"

"You may take care of Jeth for me." I kissed both her cheeks. "I thank you, Mother."

Jeth and I had said our farewells at the lambing pen, but as I walked out to join my brother, I hesitated and turned to embrace him once more. Between us, my belly tightened, and in that moment I somehow knew that I was carrying his son.

I would not tell him this. Not when I could not know if I would live to give birth to Jeth's child. Instead, I framed his face with my hands and kissed him. "I shall think of you every day and night, my isi, my husband."

Tears ran down his face, but he did not bother to wipe them away. "So shall I, as I wait for your return, my isti, my wife."

CHAPTER
20

For all that I had longed to have family, and was glad to know that Barak and I shared the bond of blood, it seemed unbearable that I would have to abandon Jeth and Urlai. I missed them more with each passing hour, and was too heartsick to summon a waking dream to know if I would ever see them again. I was afraid to know that I would not, and brooding on this kept me silent as we journeyed from Ephraim into the wilderness.

Barak stopped only long enough to give the priest in the village a message to send to the tribes in the north, and receive his blessing on our journey. Then we rode miles through the mountains, often on narrow and stony roads, and camped in likely spots when the sun went down.

At night I prepared food and did what I could to make my brother and me as comfortable as possible, but even then we did not speak much beyond only the necessary words. He seemed to fall to sleep the instant we stretched out on our sleeping mats, leaving me to shed silent tears and muffle sobs as I thought of Jeth.

On the third day of our journey, Barak said, "I do not like hearing you cry yourself to sleep."

"I miss my husband," I said. My voice, so long silent, sounded like the gravel crunching under the pack animals' hooves.

"I miss my wife, too. You could speak more and keep my thoughts from wandering," my brother complained. "I begin to think you dislike me."

"I hardly know you well enough to like or dislike you," I replied, "and you have not much to say for yourself."

"I have never had a sister. I suppose I am better at issuing orders to soldiers." He was silent for a time, and then he asked, "What is he like? Our father?"

"I am a truth-seer," I warned him. "I cannot tell you pretty lies about Ybyon. Indeed, I would rather not tell you anything about him at all."

"It is probably for the best. But I look like him a little, do I not?" He rubbed his chin. "I must, for I do not resemble my mother or her kin."

"You have the best of his looks." I remembered my former master's harsh features, and tried to think of something about him that would not disgust my brother. "He was not entirely a bad man. He showed much devotion to his Canaanite family. He saw to it that they always had the best of things."

"While my mother had to marry a man she did not love to avoid shame after he raped her, and you were treated like a dog," Barak said, the same pleasant note in his voice that our father affected when he wished to cover his rage.

"We cannot choose who sires us," I reminded him. "I am glad that we have found each other."

"You are?"

"I grew up alone, with only other slaves as friends, and no family to call my own." I smiled at him. "I always thought it would be a happy thing to have a brother or sister."

"We find each other on the brink of a war, which you must foresee and I must lead." My brother shook his head. "Sometimes I think I will never understand the will of Jehovah."

That conversation seemed to end most of the tension between us, and we spoke casually after that. I did not say much of my life in Hazor, but I told Barak tales of Syman and Imen, and the wedding feast Jeth's family had given for us. I also described the river journey we had taken to Ephraim, and what I had seen along the way.

"I do miss the fish the bargemen cooked for us," I admitted. "Though I will never say so to Jeth. He was worried the whole journey that I might stay behind and take a bargeman for husband."

In turn, Barak told me a little of his life in the north country. As tribal leader, he had to direct many things, but made time to spend with his wife and their children. I was pleased to know that I had two nephews and a niece in Kedesh.

"Tere, my daughter, looks much like you. I thought that the first time I saw your face," my brother informed me. "I imagine your children will share some of my looks."

"That is the way of it," I agreed, and touched my stomach with my hand.

Barak stared at me. "You are with child? Now?"

"I think I may be." I rubbed a circle over the flatness beneath it. "I will not know for another moon."

"I already have enough to worry me," my brother grumbled. "Now I will be fearing for your unborn."

We came to the place where the tribes would assemble, and went about setting up camp. By nightfall men from the northern tribes began to arrive, and Barak attended to them while I saw to the food and supplies that came on the wagons with them.

It took only another two days before a force of ten thousand men had gathered and were ready to march.

Barak was so busy, he rarely ate and hardly slept. As the only woman in camp, I stayed out of the way by confining myself to his tent, tending his fire and preparing his meals. He left one afternoon when reports of a skirmish nearby came to him, and did not return until well past nightfall.

I was stirring the pot of soup I was keeping warm when my brother stepped into the tent. He was still wearing his leather battle armor, and carried a sword. I did not look at the blood on his weapon or the weariness in his face. Instead, I prepared his tea and carried it to him in silence.

He did not wish to speak to me, either, but after a time the words came from him, low and angry. "They were common raiders, paid by Sisera to attack Hebrew settlements. They took two farms to the south before we reached them. They killed all the livestock and butchered the families. Even the children were not spared."

My stomach, already tight with nerves, rolled. "I am sorry that you had to see that."

He reclined on the fine pillows provided for the rest he never took. "My mother said the truth is never easy. Neither is death."

The next day the army broke camp, and we began the long march to Mount Tabor. I rode with my brother at the front of the troops, and as it was the first time many of the men had caught sight of me, we received many curious looks. I did not encourage the officers who rode beside my brother to speak to me, and I kept myself modestly veiled during the hours we marched. The last thing the men needed now was a distraction or a reminder of the wives and mothers they had left behind.

Mount Tabor rose from the center of its surrounding plains, a steep and rather ugly-looking sight as we came down from the hills toward it. I could see the wisdom of Jehovah in choosing this as our base, for Sisera's chariots would find no purchase on the steep slopes. There were many caves, natural stone shelves and other niches where our men could repel any infantry attacks while easily defend their own positions.

The work of moving the army up the mountain and settling them in place required a full day of hard effort, for weapons, supplies, and food had to be carried on the men's backs as they climbed. Once above the base, however, the slope of the ground decreased and offered many places of rest for the tired troops.

Barak set up his command center in the largest cave, and had me ensconced in a small chamber at the back with his weapons and food. He himself spread out my sleeping mat and ordered me to sleep.

"I can make my own meal this night," he told me when I argued, "and you look ready to collapse. Go and sleep, sister, for tomorrow I will need your counsel."

The men from the southern tribes had not yet arrived as promised, and I wondered if the old village priest had delivered my message to the leaders in Rameh. Then I worried that the leaders might have changed their minds and decided not to send their troops.

We cannot fight the Canaanites with only ten thousand men, I thought as I drifted off to sleep. *They will overwhelm the sentries and come up over the mountain like a swarm of ants.*

The dream that came to me that night was not of Jeth or my brother, but of the farm I had left behind in Hazor.

I walked past the empty barn and saw the pasture grass had grown very tall. There was no sign of the flocks, or any farmworkers. The main house, too, appeared abandoned, and I would have thought myself completely alone had I not spotted a lone man standing beyond the fleece shed, working the soil with a long-handled spade.

Thinking it might be Meji or Tarn or one of the others, I hurried toward the man. Only when I drew close did I see it was my former master, working to fill in the brimming, odorous pit of a well-used privy.

I backed up a step, but a twig snapped under my sandal, and Ybyon looked up at me. He was thin now, and his skin had turned bright red from working under the sun. Someone had shaved the hair from his scalp, leaving only sparse stubble, and upon his brow were scabbed-over marks, the brands given to thieves and murderers.

"My daughter Deborah." He smiled, dropped the spade, and walked toward me. His body was covered with filth and flies from the privy, and on his hips he wore only an old threadbare ezor tied with some twine. "It has been too long. Why do you frown? Are you not happy to see me?"

"I am not." I turned and tried to run, but my legs would not move.

"In my nightmares, I see your face, almost every night now," Ybyon said in his most pleasant voice. "I wake up crying out for my wife. I cannot see her anymore, for she was sold as a concubine to a fat sea trader. My children were torn from her and portioned off to some of my old business rivals. They are being worked to death on their farms." He grinned, showing broken teeth. "Just as you were on mine."

I turned slowly around and faced the ugliness of my father. "I did not do this to them. By your crimes, you did."

"Of course I did." He chuckled, and reached out to give my cheek a hard pinch. "I do not deny that. I deny nothing. Well, I did deny you a mother, and refused to see you as my daughter, but that is all in the past. You forgave me my sins, remember?" He began to laugh, a horrible, wrenching noise. "You forgave me. Do you know, that is the most amusing thing anyone has ever said to me?"

I did forgive him, and I was terribly sad to see him in such a state, but I could not bear to be near him another moment. I willed my legs to move, and when they did, I ran for the barn.

"Wait, Deborah," my father called after me. "Do you not wish to give me an embrace? Your mother never denied me those. She made herself my whore to protect you."

He was coming after me, and I knew I could not fight him. I ran into the barn and climbed the ladder into the hayloft. There I dragged the ladder up behind me and hid in the straw as he burst through the door.

"Come out, daughter," he called. "For you cannot win against me."

I buried myself deep in the hay and prayed that God would deliver me from this evil dream.

"Ybyon," a soft voice called, silencing my father. "If you wish to hurt someone, come to me. I am here."

"Dasah?" My father turned around as if looking for her. "Where are you, you lying witch?"

"I am where you left me to die," my mother called. "Outside in the pens. Would you like me to see your future now?"

Ybyon cursed and ran out of the barn. I was swept from the hayloft by a terrible wind, but I landed on the ground below like a feather. I bolted outside to see my mother standing in the pen among the lambs where she had been killed, and my father climbing over the fence to get at her.

"Mother!" I shouted. "*No.*"

Dasah opened her arms as if welcoming Ybyon, who rushed at her like a mad dog. Between them the ground turned to mud, and Ybyon became caught in it and could no longer move. The mud widened and seemed to suck him down deep into the ground, inch by slow inch. He struggled and bellowed, but no matter what he did, he could not free himself.

"This is what you and your brother must do, my daughter," Dasah said, her body fading from sight even as my father was dragged under the mud, his last scream swallowed just as he was. "This is how you shall prevail over the enemy."

I woke up at that moment and saw my brother kneeling beside my mat. He was shaking my shoulders.

"Deborah, you were calling out for me." He helped me to sit up and gave me a cup of water. "Sisera's forces have arrived. They are encamped around the base of the mountain, but they cannot get to us. The southern tribes have sent their ten thousand, and they are just beyond the river, as you said." He patted my back awkwardly. "I am sorry that I woke you so abruptly. Were you having a nightmare?"

"Yes." I drank deeply before I spoke again. "And no. I have finally seen the end of this, and I know what to do now."

"What is it?"

I rose from my mat. "Come and I will show you."

The history scrolls would all tell the story of the next three days, in which my brother repelled Sisera from Mount Tabor, and the frustrated Canaanites were forced to wait below, helpless to draw us out, unable to attack us.

I waited for the final sign to be shown in the heavens before I left my brother on the mountain. "When the chariots head toward the Kishon, then it will be time to descend," I told him as I dressed.

"I am putting my faith in you and God," Barak said. "But if one of you is wrong, they shall turn back, and we shall be done for."

"Have faith, brother," I urged him.

I selected two of his trusted lieutenants to escort me to the river, but I took no weapons with me. As I prepared to leave, I joined my brother at his lookout spot, which showed most of the Canaanite army encamped at the base of the mountain. They had brought some captured Hebrew settlers with them, and had resorted to torturing them in the open, hoping to draw down some of my brother's troops.

"I will be glad to get my hands on Sisera," Barak muttered. "Before this is over, I want his head adorning my tent pole." He took my hand in his. "Be careful, sister."

"It will not be you who brings Sisera to the justice he deserves," I said as a brief vision settled over me. "For God soon delivers him into the hands of a woman who shall slay him."

Barak smiled. "You will kill him for me?"

I shook myself and tried not to look at the heavy dark clouds massing over us. "No, and watch your pride, brother, that it does not make you fall from this mountain."

There was no way to leave the mountain without Sisera's troops spotting us, but I wanted them to see me. So with my brother's men I ran out of the brush and through the least concentrated area of camp, moving so fast that by the time Sisera's men realized I had come through, we were already past them.

"Here is General Barak, and he cannot be caught by a Canaanite even when he runs through the midst of their camp," one of the men with me called back in a taunting voice. "Nor do they see us leaving the mountain in the night when they are sleeping. Let us see if they can catch us at the river before we sail to freedom."

The race was on. We could not stop now, for Sisera and his army gave chase, and we had to reach the Kishon before they did. I had never run so far or so fast, but my legs never faltered, and at last we reached the edge of the swampy land where the southern tribes had crossed the river and were camped.

"Sisera and his armies are coming," the men with me shouted out. "Prepare to fight, but stay to the river side of the swamp."

The southern forces were armed and ready, as they had been ordered to be, and spread out along the banks of the river. I retreated to a tree where I could see Sisera's thousand iron chariots approaching from the base of Mount Tabor.

"They are almost here," I called down to one of my men.

At that moment the black masses of clouds overhead began to shower heavy, pounding sheets of rain over us, making it impossible to see more than a few feet in every direction. I could hear the chariots slowing as they came to the swamp and then the shouts of their drivers as their heavy iron wheels met with the water and thick mud being made by the downpour.

Within minutes the sounds of the chariots were gone, and the shouts turned to battle cries as the Canaanites abandoned them and rushed on foot toward the river. They had almost reached our men there when another, more ominous sound came from behind Sisera's troops.

It was the sound of ten thousand more men; my brother and his troops, who had followed Sisera into the swamp.

I had dreamed of battles, but the reality was an ugly and hideous thing. The Canaanites, trapped between the southern tribes at the river and my brother's troops coming from Mount Tabor, were caught completely off-guard. The storm had ripped away the battle superiority of their iron chariots, and the dense showers blinded their infantry.

Many hours later, when it was finally over, most of Sisera's army lay dead in the swamp. Sisera himself escaped on foot, but I had foreseen his end, and knew he would not enjoy his freedom long.

My brother came to stand beneath the

tree where I had been sitting most of that long, terrible day. He was covered in blood and gore, some of it from the wounds that marked his arms and legs. "Deborah, come down from there."

I climbed down the tree and stood before him.

"It was as you said it would be. Everything was." He went down on one knee before me and bowed his head, and suddenly every man around us did the same. "Bless you for saving us, sister."

I had cried so much while watching and listening to the battle that my eyes were almost swollen shut. I wiped the last of my tears from my cheeks and asked him, "Have we won?"

"Yes." He stood, and smiled down at me. "Israel is grateful for this victory, lady."

"Thank the Lord God."

"Our people are saved because of you, Deborah." He touched my cheek. "Ask anything of me, and I will make it yours."

I turned away from the sight of the battlefield. Jehovah's will had been done, and now I wanted only one thing for myself. "May I go home to my husband now?"

* * *

When the wagon finally reached the farm road, I asked my brother to stop and let me walk the rest of the way.

"Everyone is sleeping by now," I said, "and I do not wish to startle them. I will just slip inside. You are welcome to stay with us, too."

"I am eager to go home to my wife," Barak told me. "Now that there will be peace, I think I may raise some sheep and goats. After all you told me about caring for them on the journey here, I think I may be an expert." He climbed down and embraced me.

"I shall see you in the spring, as you promised me, and you are to bring everyone with you." I hugged him close. "Your wife, and my nephews and niece, and anyone else who would make the journey. We have room enough for them all."

"I will send word as soon as the snows melt." He kissed my brow. "God watch over you, sister."

It was a long walk up to the house, but I was happy to cross land that was not stained with blood, or strewn with the bodies of dead soldiers. As we had left the swamp at Kishon, I had seen the body of Hlagor, Ybyon's steward, dressed in a Canaanite uniform. He had been dragged out from an overturned chariot, and the rain had scoured the mud that he had drowned in from his face.

The wind was not so cold here as it had been in the north, but I kept the furs my brother had given me wrapped around me as I approached the house. There I saw a single lamp burning, and someone seated in a chair by the door. It was my husband, dozing by the lamp, in the chair where he had been sitting and watching the road.

I went to him and covered him with my furs, and as he opened his eyes I leaned over and blew out the flame of the oil lamp.

"Deborah." He looked at me with drowsy surprise. "You are here." He pulled me down onto his lap and held me close. "I fell asleep. I was just sitting here and watching the night and thinking that I should have carried you off during that hailstorm."

"I think you should have," I agreed, snuggling against him.

"You feel real to me." He ran his hands over me. "You *are* here—or do I dream?"

"If this is a dream," I said before I kissed him, as I had on our wedding night, "let us never wake."

Discussion Guide

1. Human slavery dates back before recorded history, and only began to be universally abolished three hundred years ago. There are still some countries whose long-established cultures and customs perpetuate enslavement, especially for ethnic and religious minorities. Should more liberal countries take direct action to wipe out modern-day slavery in such societies? When, if ever, is enslavement justified?

2. Deborah has the gift of prophecy, and she uses it to help her people. What

would it be like to have such an extraordinary power? If you had such a gift, would you conceal it, or use it? Discuss what the consequences might be.

3. Ybyon, the Canaanite farmer who owns Deborah, lost most of his family during the fall of Jericho. This results in his hatred of Hebrews, his abuse of his slaves, and ultimately his plot to rob and murder Jeth Lappidoth, a Hebrew merchant. How does Ybyon's situation compare to that of other vengeful figures from the Bible? Does suffering tremendous personal loss entitle someone to take revenge?

4. Deborah's prophetic powers elevate her to become a judge of Israel, and to direct General Barak and his army during a battle with the Canaanites. Yet Deborah lived during a time period when women were never permitted to serve as government and military leaders. Why do you think God chose to give Deborah the gift of prophecy when He could have bestowed it on a man? Can women function as well as men in positions of authority? Should women have

the same opportunity as men to provide spiritual guidance to others?

5. Barak believes in Deborah's power of prophecy so implicitly that he refuses to go into battle without her leading his army. What do you think inspired him to put such faith in a former slave? Should so many men's lives be entrusted to experienced strategists, or to inspired visionaries?

6. Doubt and fear plague Deborah throughout her story, and yet when she is called upon to serve God and her people, she willingly puts herself in danger to save others. In today's world, terrorists and other extremists pose a constant threat to everyone. What do you find threatening about living in this time? How do you cope with your doubts and fears? If you had to risk your life to save many others, would you feel willing or obligated to do so?

7. The Book of Judges tells how some Israeli losses during their war with the Canaanites were God's punishment for violation of holy law. Do you believe God only favors the righteous during war-

time? Are there parallels between the ancient invasion of Canaan and more modern invasions?

8. Barak and Deborah faced Sisera's army, which was supported by soldiers driving nine hundred iron chariots. The Hebrews, who had no chariots, were at a distinct disadvantage, and yet with the help of God and nature, they prevailed over the Canaanites. What are some other instances in history when chance seemingly turned the tide of battle? How significant a role does weather play during warfare?

9. Despite all the suffering and deprivation Ybyon inflicted on his slaves, and the fact that he murdered Deborah's mother, Deborah chooses to forgive her former master. Would you be able to do the same? How can we extend the same kind of forgiveness to the people who cause us the most harm?

10. The ancient Hebrews invaded Canaan on the strength of a belief: that God had given them the land by divine right. Three thousand years later, their de-

scendants are still fighting with the descendants of the ancient Canaanites over the "Promised Land." Do you believe this ongoing dispute will ever be settled peacefully? Does faith justify using displacement and violence to settle territorial feuds?

Glossary

Author's note: The terms used in this novel were derived from Hebrew and Canaanite. I have removed certain punctuation and spelled them in such a way to make them reader-friendly.

adasim: lentils
Adon: a term of respect for a man, lord, or
     master
bayit: literally "house," place of business
bet bama: a shrine or holy place
ezor: a kiltlike garment worn by men
gerum: outcasts
hagora: a belt used to hold the ezor in place

hereb: a sword
himmesim: chick peas
hitta: wheat
isi: husband
isti: wife
keli: jewel
kesut: outer robe
kuttonet: tuniclike boy's garment
massebot: standing stones
middo: a tuniclike garment
pol: fava beans
qali: parched grain
qemah: flour
seba: literally "gray head," used as a casual
    address for an older man
shofar: trumpet
simla: kiltlike garment
siqma: sycamore
tahan: meal made of ground grain
ugot: grain cakes
zaqen: literally "elder," used as an address of
    respect toward a superior or older man
zetim: olives

Recommended Reading

Herzog, Chaim, and Mordecai Gichon. *Battles of the Bible*. Mechanicsburg, PA: Greenhill Books/Lionel Leventhal Limited, 2002.

Potok, Chaim. *Wanderings: Chaim Potok's History of the Jews*. New York: Fawcett Books, 1990.

Sawyer, John F. A. *Prophecy and the Biblical Prophets*. New York: Oxford University Press, 1993.

Weems, Renita J. *Battered Love: Marriage, Sex, and Violence in the Hebrew Prophets*. Minneapolis: Augsburg Fortress, 1995.